★★★★★★★★★★★★★★★★★★★★★★★★★★★★★★

little
FOOTBALL
BIG LEAGUERS™

★★

Bruce Nash and Allan Zullo
Compiled by Tom Muldoon

LITTLE SIMON
Published by Simon & Schuster Inc.
NEW YORK LONDON TORONTO SYDNEY TOKYO SINGAPORE

ACKNOWLEDGMENTS

We wish to thank all the players' parents, relatives, friends, and former coaches for generously helping us obtain childhood photographs. Among others who were kind enough to help in our photo search were Richard Alvarez, Dale and Jean Baker, John Blackshear, William Brogan, Candice Federico, Julien Grakul, Valerie Ivery, Irene Mehaffy, Ed Nestor, Kit Redeker, and Jim Semon.

We are grateful to the following reporters who contributed valuable player interviews: Bill Althaus, Phil Anastasia, Rich Beall, Jarrett Bell, John Clayton, Andy Cohen, John Crumpacker, Tim Dutton, Peter Finney, Larry Fitzgerald, Tom Ford, Tom Friend, Hank Gola, Kris Kort, David Little, Kevin Mannix, John McClain, Bob McManaman, Todd Melloh, Milt Northrop, Mike Paolercio, Dan Pompei, Jeff Schudel, Jimmy Smith, Curt Sylvester, and Rick Weinberg.

We also appreciate the help we received from Julio Mateus and the public relations offices of the NFL teams.

PHOTO CREDITS

Cover: Tom DiPace—Singletary, Elway; Miami Dolphins—Marino; Jerry Pinkus—Simms. All other action photos and head shots of the players came from the teams except for the following: DiPace—Carter, Stark, Browner; Robert L. Smith—Reed; Scott Cunningham—Mann; Denny Landwehr—Munoz; Bill Amatucci—C. Wolfley; Michael Fabus—Ilkin.

In order to publish this book for the start of the 1990 football season, it was necessary to finish it by the spring of 1990. As a result, the book does not reflect any change of teams that a player might have made since the completion of the manuscript.

Little Simon
Simon & Schuster Building, Rockefeller Center
1230 Avenue of the Americas, New York, New York 10020

10 9 8 7 6 5 4 3 2 1

ISBN: 0-671-70850-3

★★★★★★★★★★★★★★★★★★★★★

To Mom and Dad, for giving me the
chance to pursue my dreams.
B.N.

To the Arnold and Linquist
clans—Eleanor, Greg, Steve, and Barb;
and Kay and Dwight—who've never
grown up, the lucky stiffs.
A.Z.

To my wife, Kathy, who has faith that this
will be the first of many.
T.M.

You probably know a lot about your favorite NFL stars from watching them play on television or from reading about them in magazines and the sports pages. It's likely you know almost everything about them from the number of yards they rushed last Sunday to the number of interceptions they made last season.

But chances are you've read very little, if anything, about the stars' playing days when they were kids. That's what *little FOOTBALL BIG LEAGUERS* is all about. Here you will find amazing boyhood stories of today's pro football players along with previously unseen photos of them as kids.

We talked to quarterbacks, running backs, linemen, kickers, All-Pros, and rookies about their days playing football as kids. When we approached the players, they were delighted to share stories about their early days growing up on the gridiron. Many of the players revealed their treasured boyhood experiences for the very first time.

Some stories are funny, others are inspiring; some are fascinating, others are embarrassing. For instance, All-Pro tackle Anthony Munoz of the Cincinnati Bengals laughed as he recounted the time he was playing flag football in the eighth grade. He was running with the ball when a defender grabbed hold of Anthony's shorts and pulled them down—in front of the whole student body!

As kids, players took up football for the zaniest reasons. Dallas Cowboys quarterback Troy Aikman said he went out for football in fourth grade because he fell in love with a seventh-grade cheerleader and wanted to get her attention. Bennie Blades, of the Detroit Lions, said he decided to play football because it was safer than staying home with his older sister. She used to hit him over the head with her tap dancing shoes whenever he didn't do his chores.

Mothers played a big role in many of the players' stories. Green Bay Packers wide receiver Perry Kemp said that when he broke loose on a long run, his mother would run step for step with him along the sidelines. Steve Young, quarterback of the San Francisco 49ers, said his mother once came charging onto the field to scold a boy who had just tackled him around the neck. "I was so embarrassed I wouldn't let her go to my games after that," Steve said with a laugh.

In addition to the players themselves, relatives and former coaches told their sides of the stories as well. They also helped us obtain photos of the stars as children. These photos accompany the stories in this book and they also appear on the *little FOOTBALL BIG LEAGUERS* trading cards in the special bonus section in the back.

Perhaps when you read the book, you'll identify with some of the experiences—both good and bad—that these players had in their youth. Who knows? Perhaps one day your story will appear in a book about young football players who grew up to become NFL stars.

DAN MARINO

Eight-year-old Dan Marino was too small to play for the St. Regis Vikings, the football team at the Catholic school he attended in Pittsburgh, Pennsylvania. Although the fourth grader showed promise as a budding quarterback, he was cut. He just couldn't compete with older boys, many of whom were eighth graders.

Instead of being upset that he couldn't play, the future Miami Dolphins' All-Pro quarterback figured out a way to join the team—he made himself the water boy. "I just wanted to be part of the team," said Dan. "I didn't care what I did as long as I got to wear a Vikings shirt during games."

Football wasn't new to Dan. He'd been playing with his dad, Dan Marino, Sr., ever since he was old enough to hold a football. His dad worked nights, driving a truck for the *Pittsburgh Press*. "Dan insisted that we play catch every night before I went to work," said Dan Sr. "He'd throw the foot-

ball to me hundreds of times. He was just a little fellow, but you could see he had promise as a quarterback. He could really throw the ball."

Dan's father helped coach the Vikings. Every day during football season, young Dan tagged along to practice with his dad. Finally, when Dan was eight, he tried out for the team, but he was cut. "Dan was heartbroken," said Dan Sr. "He loved the Vikings and wanted to be a member very badly. Unfortunately, he was just too small and he was competing against much older boys with better developed talent. Dan was told that he'd have to wait until he was in fifth grade to try out again. But unlike many other boys, Dan wasn't destroyed by this rejection. He was determined to be part of the team."

Instead of staying home and moping, Dan continued to go to practice every day with his father. He played catch on the sidelines with team members. Then he figured out a way to get a Vikings jersey.

Recalled Dan Sr., "It was a very hot day, and the team took a break in the middle of the field. Suddenly, Dan came running out with a bucket filled with water. He just started handing out cupfuls of water to the players. No one told him to do it. He decided to do it on his own. From that moment on, Dan became the official water boy of the team."

When the coaches saw Dan's dedication to the team, they presented him with the thing he wanted the most—a Vikings jersey. It was slightly tattered and well used. "The jersey was too big for him," said Dan's father. "It hung down to his knees and had a few holes in it, too. But Dan didn't care. He was so thrilled to wear the jersey with the green number 24 on it that you couldn't get the smile off his face."

So for the rest of the year, the boy who would one day break many of the passing records in the National Football League was happy to be a water boy just so he could be part of the team.

The next year, Dan made the Vikings as a third-string quarterback. He only played on extra point attempts and didn't get to throw the ball. Said his dad, "Dan was small, so on extra points, he would take the snap and run behind the bigger linemen until he saw a hole. Then he'd head for the end zone. Dan scored a lot of extra points that way because the other team just couldn't see him behind our linemen."

In sixth grade, Dan moved up to second string. Then, in seventh and eighth grade, Dan became an all-star quarterback. He led the team, on which he was once the water boy, to back–to–back city championships.

Running
Back
―――
San
Francisco
49ers

★ ★ ★

When San Francisco 49ers running back Roger Craig played defense as a young boy, he was so scared of getting hurt that he wouldn't tackle the ball carrier. Roger was simply a wimp on the football field.

"I hated to be hit," Roger admitted. "I'd do anything to keep from getting hit. I was a real crybaby."

Roger started playing football when he was eight years old in the Pee Wee League in Davenport, Iowa. He was a wide receiver on offense and a linebacker on defense. "Offense was great," Roger recalled. "All I wanted to do was catch the ball. I scored almost every time I caught a pass because I was so scared of getting hit that I wouldn't let anyone touch me. I'd just catch the ball and run like crazy."

Unfortunately for Roger, his team had few members so he had to play defense, too. "I didn't like defense because I didn't want to get hurt," Roger said. "My coach stuck me at left outside linebacker, but I wouldn't tackle anybody. I was too scared to hit a runner. I told my teammates that if the play came my way, I was heading the other way."

Roger's coach, Tom Rodriguez, used to scream at Roger to make the tackle, but Roger would just dodge the ball carrier. The coach was also upset with Roger on offense. He felt Roger deliberately didn't catch some passes when there was a defender near him because Roger feared getting hit.

Finally, the coach had an idea. He threatened to tell Roger's older brother, Curtis, who was a big high school star, that Roger was afraid to hit or get hit. "Coach Rodriguez said that he'd get Curtis to come out to our practices and run over me until I stopped him," Roger recalled. "Since Curtis was an All-State running back and he was much bigger than me, I knew I could never stop him. Besides, I didn't want my brother to think I was a coward. So I started hitting, but I didn't like it very much."

Although Curtis knew about Roger's fear of being hit, he never said anything to his younger brother, according to their mother, Ernestine. "Curtis used to take Roger out in the alley and play football with him. He'd throw the ball as hard as he could and make Roger catch it. Then he'd run at half-speed and make Roger tackle him. Curtis helped Roger get tougher, but he did it in a gentle way. Roger wouldn't quit. He wanted to be a winner. Once he got over his fear of being hit, he just kept getting better and better."

Fear was a big obstacle for Roger to overcome. But he felt that he had to do it in order to stay on the football team. "I loved playing," Roger said. "I loved having teammates. To remain a part of the team and play the game I loved, I had to overcome my fear. Many young football players are afraid of being hit, but if I could learn to take it, then anyone can learn. Fear can be conquered. I became a better person and a better football player when I learned that lesson."

ROHN STARK

Twelve-year-old Rohn Stark felt so much pressure during his first year of playing organized football that he couldn't remember in what direction each play was supposed to go. Since he was the quarterback, this was a big flaw. Finally, he had to write the directions of each running play on his hands!

Before the All-Pro punter for the Indianapolis Colts played his first down of organized football, he competed in the national Punt, Pass and Kick contest. As a ten-year-old, Rohn won the local competition in Pine River, Minnesota. Two years later, as the quarterback on his seventh-grade team, Rohn thought he could easily handle the pressure of his position. But in his first game, he found out he was wrong.

"I came up with total brain lock," he recalled. "I knew all the plays because I had practiced them a hundred times. But the first time I called a running play in an actual game, the pressure got to me. I turned right to hand off to a halfback going through the hole. The only problem was that the halfback was going through the left side of the line."

In most play-calling systems, each of the holes on an offensive line is numbered. Usually the odd numbers are to the left of center and the even numbers are to the right. So if a back's number is called through the 2 hole, the back should run between the center and the guard on the right side of the line. Unfortunately, when the chips were down, Rohn couldn't remember where the 2 hole was.

"Under pressure and on the spur of the

moment, I used to forget which was my right, and which was my left," he admitted. "For the quarterback, that was fatal. Passing plays weren't bad because I could visually correct any mistakes I made. On running plays, I was always turning the wrong way and there would be nobody to hand off to."

The coach came up with a solution. He had Rohn write between his fingers the number of the hole through which each running play was designed to go. "The coach had me write the odd numbers on my left hand between my fingers," said Rohn. "I wrote the even numbers between my fingers on my right hand. That way I knew where the hole was. If I called a back through the 4 hole, I'd look at my hand and see the 4 between my middle finger and

the next finger on my right hand. I'd know exactly where to hand off. When the weather turned cold, the coach had me paint the numbers on my gloves. I played through the whole seventh grade using this system."

After that year, Rohn became accustomed to the pressure and he didn't need to write the numbers on his hands anymore. But his running backs never trusted him at quarterback. "They thought that I'd forget where they were going," he said.

To this day, Rohn, who has survived many key pressure plays in pro football, is still kidded by his friends back home in Pine River. "I'll never outlive it," he said. "To my friends, I'll always be the guy who couldn't remember the plays in pressure situations."

MIKE SINGLETARY

Mike Singletary was given one game to prove he could play football. If he didn't do well, he would have to give up the game and work after school for his father in the construction business.

"My dad gave me one chance when I was in the seventh grade," recalled the Chicago Bears' All-Pro middle linebacker. "He didn't want me wasting time in a sport unless I could play it well."

Mike's parents refused to allow him to play organized football in grade school because their religion didn't allow its members to participate in sports. His parents were devout Pentecostals—and his dad was a preacher. "I always wanted to play football, but my parents wouldn't give me permission," Mike recalled. "I used to sneak away when I was in grade school and play with the kids in the park. If my parents had found out, I would have been punished."

As Mike's love for the game grew, he began to have desperate thoughts. "When I was in the seventh grade, I brought home a letter of agreement for my father to sign that would allow me to play football. If he didn't sign it, I was going to run away and live with my married sister."

Mike was afraid when he asked his father to sign the letter of agreement. "I want to play," Mike pleaded. "I was born to play football." Something in Mike's face made his father believe him. To Mike's astonishment, his dad agreed to sign the permission slip. "He told me that he was giving me one chance," Mike recalled. "He said that if I didn't play my first game well, then I would have to come work with him after school at his construction business."

So Mike went out for football at Crispus Attucks Junior High School in Houston, Texas. But he was far behind his teammates, who had been playing organized football for several years. As a result, he was assigned to the junior varsity team where he became a second stringer.

Mike was worried on the day of his first game against Sharptown Junior High. He didn't know if he would get to play at all, let alone prove to his dad that he could play well. Mike's older brother, Grady, was assigned to watch the game and report back on Mike's performance. "I was really scared," Mike recalled. "Late in the fourth quarter, I was still sitting on the bench. I hadn't been in for one play. We were getting smashed by Sharptown and our coach was angry."

Frustrated with the play of his middle linebacker, the coach turned to Mike on the bench and ordered him into the game. "I was excited and scared," Mike said. "I didn't think I was going to get a chance to play. I knew Grady was watching and had to report my progress back to my dad. My whole football career depended on how well I did."

On the next play from scrimmage, Sharptown's huge fullback ran into the middle of the line. Mike came up quickly and crashed into the runner, but hardly slowed him down. "I hit him hard," Mike said. "He just ran right over me, but I managed to hold onto an ankle. He dragged me for ten yards, then shook me off, and broke loose for a touchdown. I was lying in the dirt, tears running down my cheeks, as I watched him run into the end zone. I thought all my dreams of playing football were gone."

The defense never returned to the field, so Mike didn't get another chance to play that day. Dejected, he walked home with his brother thinking he'd never play again. "Halfway home I couldn't stand it any longer," Mike said. "I asked Grady what he was going to tell Dad. Grady said, 'I'm going to tell him that you did your very best, Mike.' I stood speechless and just looked at my brother. Then I hugged him."

Grady's testimony satisfied Mike's father and Mike went on to become a star in junior and senior high school before earning All-America honors at Baylor University.

"My parents became my greatest fans," Mike said. "And my religion never suffered. I believe that any human being can serve the Lord by doing what he does best. The Lord made me to be a football player."

MIKE LANSFORD

Mike Lansford had such severe pain in his right leg that he couldn't use it to kick field goals in an important high school game. So the future Los Angeles Rams' placekicker simply shifted to his left foot and booted a game-winning 37-yard field goal.

Seventeen-year-old Mike was in his senior year with the Arcadia (California) High School Apaches when he came down with a severe sciatic nerve problem that created tremendous pain through his lower back, buttocks, and right leg. "I developed it playing soccer," Mike recalled. "By the time football season came around, I was hurting so badly that I couldn't practice."

Mike had to undergo physical therapy, take anti-inflammatory medicine, and wear a corset to school. "The worse thing was that I had Ben Gay on me all of the time," he said. "You could smell me coming down the hallway. It really was a terrible senior year."

Because of his injury, Mike didn't practice with the Apaches, but he did play in games as their punter and placekicker. Usually the treatment would make his pain bearable by game time each week, so he could kick right-footed as he normally did. Except once. Mike's nerve problem flared up in the cool air of a night game against the rival Alhambra Moors. "I could punt normally because that didn't involve a twisting motion," he said. "But I couldn't placekick right-footed. The twisting motion of my soccer style kicking aggravated the pain too much."

When it became obvious that he couldn't use his normal kicking foot, he told his coach, Dick Salter, that he was going to use his other foot. Since he was a soccer player, Mike was confident that he could kick with his left foot. The coach told him to go ahead. "I kicked left-footed during the pregame warm-ups," Mike recalled. "I made about half my attempts."

In the game, Mike was called on to punt

six times. He did it right-footed, and even booted a 70-yarder—his longest punt of the year. With the score 0-0, Coach Salter sent Mike in to attempt a 37-yard field goal. "It felt odd lining up on the left side," Mike said. "When the snap came and the holder set the ball, I stepped forward and kicked the ball. I didn't really follow through. I just sort of aimed the ball." To the Apaches' joy, it cleared the crossbar! Mike had put his team up 3-0. "Everyone was surprised, including me," Mike recalled. "I was very happy to make it. I felt very awkward kicking it. It was amazing that it went through the goal posts."

Later in the game, Mike attempted an extra point left-footed, but it was blocked. Although his team won 9-0, Mike never again attempted to kick with his left foot in a game.

More memorable to Mike than his left-footed field goal was the embarrassment he felt at halftime. Because Mike's pain was so obvious, the coach ordered the team's student trainer to attend to Mike at halftime. The overzealous trainer had Mike take his pants down and proceeded to massage Mike's buttocks in front of the whole team. "It was embarrassing," Mike recalled. "We were in the small visitors' dressing room. The team was on the left side of the room, and the coach's blackboard was on the right. There I was in the center getting my butt massaged."

Mike heard lots of laughter and wise-cracks from his teammates during his massage. "No one was listening to the coach," Mike said. "They were all making fun of me. I didn't feel very macho listening to some of my teammates' comments."

While his buddies have forgotten his valiant effort to play left-footed, they have never forgotten his public butt massage. "I can't go anywhere around town without someone reminding me," Mike said. "I guess you can say I'll always be the butt of their jokes."

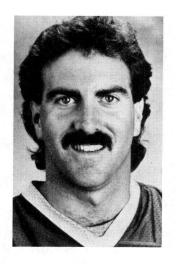

PHIL SIMMS

New York Giants quarterback Phil Simms had to be talked into playing organized football when he was a kid. That's because baseball was Phil's first love. But ironically, it was baseball that led him to football.

"I was simply crazy about baseball," said Phil, who grew up in Louisville, Kentucky, where he was known as "Whitey" because his blond hair was so light. "I was a pitcher in Little League. I had a pretty strong arm, and I enjoyed striking out batters.

"Football was okay. But it was just a game to play with my five brothers for fun. I never thought about joining any organized team. I first started playing football when I was four years old. My brothers and I were watching a game on TV when one of them said, 'Let's go outside and play

football.' So I ran into my bedroom and pulled out all my socks and stuffed them under the shoulders of my shirt and made shoulder pads. Then I went out and played. But to me, football was just a fun thing to play in the yard. Baseball, on the other hand, was a sport to play in a league where you got to wear uniforms and everything."

Phil's attitude toward football changed shortly after one particular Little League game in which he pitched. Sitting in the stands was Julien Grakul, the football coach for St. Rita's Catholic Grade School, where his son, David, and Phil were classmates. The two boys played on opposing Little League teams. On this day, Phil kept striking out David. "I couldn't believe how overpowering Phil was," recalled Coach Grakul. "He was just blowing the ball past

David and his teammates. I could see that Phil had a great arm and I thought he'd make an excellent passer. But I found out he wasn't all that interested in joining the football team. Since some of Phil's friends, like David, were on my team, I asked them to tell Phil how much fun it was. They finally convinced him to come out for football."

During tryouts for St. Rita's fifth-grade team, the Mustangs, Phil discovered he was a natural passer. "He threw exceptionally well—farther than anyone for his age," said Coach Grakul. "The grade school playing fields were 40 yards wide and 70 yards long and he could throw the ball almost all the way across the width of the field on the fly. And he was accurate, too. I made him the starting quarterback and gave him a jersey with the number 19. That was the number worn by Johnny Unitas (Hall of Fame quarterback for the Baltimore Colts). I told Phil how special that number was."

Phil made a spectacular debut in his first game for St. Rita's. On his first play from scrimmage, he dropped back and threw the ball 35 yards—half the length of the gridiron—right into David Grakul's hands. Recalled Phil, "He caught it and raced into the end zone for a touchdown. I was so happy I couldn't believe it."

With Phil at quarterback, St. Rita's finished the season with a 5-2 record. The following year, he led the Mustangs to an undefeated season and the right to play in the Toy Bowl for the city championship of the Catholic grade school league. "It was a muddy day and I ran the ball a lot," recalled Phil. "I didn't complete a single pass, but we still won. I remember thinking, 'Boy, it doesn't get much better than this.'" After a 6-1 season in seventh grade, Phil started his final year in grade school with a repeat performance of his fifth grade debut. "On the first play of the season, I threw a 50-yard touchdown pass to David Grakul," recalled Phil. "It was the identical play we ran in fifth grade. I can remember those two plays like they happened yesterday."

ANTHONY CARTER

Wide Receiver

Minnesota Vikings

★ ★ ★

When Anthony Carter first tried out for the Lake Park (Florida) Packers, no one suspected that the rail-thin nine-year-old would grow up to be a dazzling All-Pro wide receiver for the Minnesota Vikings. "He had the skinniest legs, and he didn't look like a football player," recalled his Pee Wee coach, Dual South. "But when I saw him almost outrun our tailback—while running *backwards*—Anthony became our new tailback."

What he lacked in size Anthony made up in blinding speed, amazing quickness, and eye-popping natural moves. The first two times he touched the ball he scored a TD. "He took a pitchout and raced 70 yards for a touchdown," South recalled. "On the kickoff, the other team fumbled and we recovered. On the next play from scrim-

mage, Anthony scored again on a 30-yard run. I knew then he was truly gifted."

In the three years Anthony played on the team, the Lake Park Packers won all but one of their 36 games. (The only game they lost was when Anthony had hurt his leg.) One year, the team scored 409 points in 12 games and Anthony scored 314 of them, an average of more than 26 points per game. "By then," said Carter, "I had a nickname—End Zone Carter."

In one game, Anthony had scored five touchdowns by the third quarter when the opposing coach accused South of running up the score. "What really happened was that the father of one of our players promised to take Anthony to a Miami Dolphins game if he scored five touchdowns—so there was no way Anthony wan't going to get those touchdowns," said South. "When the game got out of hand and he had the five touchdowns, I pulled him out. But he couldn't sit still on the sidelines and he kept asking me if he could play some more. I put him back in as a defensive tackle, figuring there was no way he could score while playing that position. But wouldn't you know, he recovered a fumble and scored a touchdown anyway."

It wasn't long before opposing teams figured that the only way to beat the Packers was if Anthony didn't play. So they began slugging and kicking him—even biting him—in the bottom of a pileup. They tried to get him so mad that he'd take a swing at them and get thrown out of the game. "I got into a fight once and got ejected," Anthony admitted. "The defender purposely jumped offside and tackled me hard. Then as he started to get up, he shoved his hand through my face mask. So I fought back.

"After that, other teams would get one of their worst players to try and pick a fight with me. Since that kid didn't play very much, they didn't care if he got thrown out of the game—just as long as I got ejected, too."

But Anthony's teammates were instructed by Coach South that whenever Anthony began to get upset, they were to go up to him, pat him on the behind, and say, "Hold your cool, Carter, hold your cool."

From then on, Anthony always did.

JERRY BALL

Nose Tackle

Detroit Lions

★ ★ ★

Jerry Ball learned to play football one-handed because he had to use his other hand to hold up his pants.

When the Detroit Lions' star nose tackle was seven years old in Beaumont, Texas, he was already taller than most of the older kids in his neighborhood. His friends insisted that he should play football with them in the Spindletop Little League in suburban Pear Orchard. The only problem was that Jerry was too young—the league was for boys between the ages of 8 and 13. "I was so big, though, the coaches decided to make an exception," recalled Jerry. "They let me play."

Just because Jerry was big didn't mean that he thought he was as good as the older boys. "To tell the truth, I was scared silly of playing in the league," he said. "Everyone was so much older than me. I was only in the second grade and I was playing against guys who were in the eighth grade."

That wasn't the worst thing for Jerry to contend with. When he was issued his uniform, he discovered his pants were way too big. "The only pants left were these huge ones. I was big, but not that big." The coach told him that he couldn't alter the pants in any way since they would have to be used by other players in the future. He would just have to pull the drawstrings tight and hope for the best. Jerry tried using belts and other means to keep the pants up, but they didn't work. "Nothing kept my pants up when I ran. Only one method worked. I had to hold the pants up myself."

In those days, kids practiced with the same uniform that they wore during games. Jerry would run around with one hand holding his pants, and the other trying to make tackles. In all the excitement, he often forgot to hold up his pants. "There were plenty of times at practice when my pants fell down," he said. "After the first time it happened, I started wearing shorts under my uniform pants.

"When I ran with the ball, I first gripped the ball with both hands, then I immediately grabbed for my pants with my right hand. I would run down the field, holding the ball with my left hand. On defense, I held my pants up with my right hand and made tackles with my left hand."

Once, Jerry broke away for what looked like a long touchdown run. There was no one in front of him, but out of nowhere, a defender caught him from behind. "I was so surprised, I let go of my pants and they fell down," recalled Jerry. "Luckily, I was wearing shorts under my pants or else there would have been a full moon over Beaumont, Texas. As it was, I was really embarrassed."

Jerry has never lived down that moment. "It's really good to have old friends who can keep you humble," he said. "Every time I think I'm doing real good, one of my friends will remind me of my pants coming down. I may be a pro today, but to people in my Beaumont neighborhood, I'm the kid whose rear end was always coming out of his football pants."

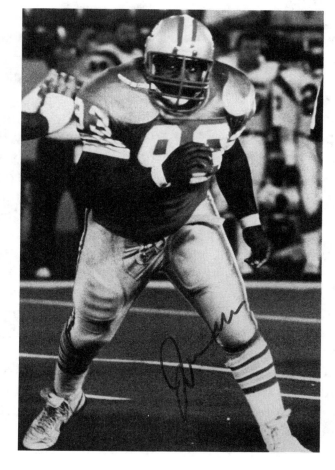

BOB GOLIC

Nose Tackle

—

Los Angeles Raiders

★ ★ ★

When Bob Golic started playing football in the fourth grade in Willwick, Ohio, he used to work harder *before* practice than he did *during* practice.

"When I arrived at practice, I'd be sweating," the future Los Angeles Raiders' nose tackle recalled. "The other kids used to think something was wrong with me." Bob had simply gone through a prepractice with his dad, Louis, who had played professional football for seven years in the Canadian Football League and who understood the game.

"I never pushed Bob into playing," his dad said. "I wanted him to have fun at whatever he chose to do. I had only one rule: If Bob started something, he had to finish it. If he wanted to play football and he didn't like it, he still had to finish out the year."

So when Bob told his dad that he was going out for the St. Mary Magdalene Elementary School Blue Angels, Louis Golic decided that he would help coach the team. "I had football experience and I knew that kids' coaches didn't always know the proper techniques," Bob's dad said. "I was determined that Bob would get good coaching."

To further train Bob for the game, his dad went out and purchased an old leather-encased blocking dummy. "The stuffing was coming out," Bob recalled. "There were rips in it, but it was still workable."

Rain or shine, for 45 minutes before practice, Bob's father would run him through drills in their backyard. Bob would hit that old blocking dummy while his father held it. "I had Bob hit the dummy over and over again," his father said. "While he did it, I coached him on the proper blocking and tackling techniques."

When it was finally time to walk down the street to practice, Bob was breathing hard and sweating heavily. He had already gone through a tougher workout than the normal practice. "My dad's prepractice in the backyard was much harder than the scheduled practice," Bob remembered. "My dad really put me through a workout."

Bob played offensive guard and defensive end for the Blue Angels. His dad's training served him well. "My dad was very supportive and made me work," Bob said. "He gave me a great foundation in the basics of football."

Bob loved the game, and he enjoyed practicing with his dad. But one day, he had a bad game and was complaining in the car. His father told him that maybe he shouldn't play football after he finished the season. "You only should play if you like football," Bob's dad told him. "After all, it's a lot of aggravation. You get cold. You get bruised and hurt. The only reason you should play the game is for yourself. If you don't enjoy it, don't play anymore."

Bob was looking for a little sympathy, but he received an important lesson instead. "I never complained to my dad about football again," Bob said. "I understood what he meant. If I truly loved the game, I had to take the bad with the good."

DINO HACKETT

Linebacker

Kansas
City
Chiefs

★ ★ ★

D ino Hackett was such a tough but clumsy boy that once during a front-yard football game, he plowed into a tree—and broke it!

When the Kansas City Chiefs' star linebacker was nine years old, he played football with his friends on the Hackett's huge front lawn in Greensboro, North Carolina. "Every weekend there was a football game played in the front yard," said his mom, Mary. "Dino was awkward so I used to watch out the window to make sure he didn't get hurt."

Mrs. Hackett planted four blue spruce trees in the yard. They were her pride and joy. "Dino and his brother Joey made me swear not to plant anything else in the yard so they would have room to play football," she said. Two trees were used as the out-of-bounds markers on one side of the field. The two other trees marked the goal lines.

"One Saturday I was playing with my friends and I caught a pass and was heading for a touchdown," Dino recalled. "I was running hard, but one of my friends had an angle on me. I tried to score just as he hit me and I went sailing into a blue spruce." Crack went the tree as Dino hit it halfway up its trunk with his shoulder. His face was scratched and bleeding. But that wasn't his chief concern. "I looked at the house first to see if my mom was looking out the window," Dino recalled. "When I didn't see her, I tried to fix the tree." Dino quickly propped the tree up and tied it together. He never told his mother that he'd broken the tree.

"A month later we all got out of the family car and my mother noticed the tree had

24

turned yellow," Dino recalled. "She asked if something was wrong with it. I ignored the question." To this day, there are only three healthy trees in the yard. The fourth is a black stump.

Dino kept another football secret from his mother. It involved a time when he and his friends played a daily game of football during recess at Sumner Elementary School. "It was tackle football and our fourth-grade teacher, Miss Taylor, didn't like us to play," Dino recalled. "She thought we were too violent." In one game, Dino accidentally tackled a boy around the neck. The boy hit the ground hard and was hurt. "Miss Taylor came tearing across the school yard," Dino said. "She took one look at the injured boy and I was banned from ever playing football at recess again. I never told my mother about my being banned."

Finally, when Dino was old enough to play organized football, his mom signed him up. "He was so anxious," she recalled. "He couldn't wait to start practicing. But

he was still awkward and he stumbled around a lot."

The first agility drill that Dino had to perform called for him to run backward along a 50-foot length of wire fence. "He couldn't do it," his mom said. "He was so awkward that he kept falling down." Dino felt crushed because he couldn't do this simple drill. "All my friends were watching me make a fool of myself," he recalled. "I became very nervous and I started throwing up. My mom had to come down to the field and help me." She put her arm around Dino and comforted him. "He wanted to quit because he couldn't run backward," she said. "He always wanted to do everything perfectly. I told him that he'd learn to do it. Then I told him to get back out there."

In time, Dino became more coordinated and went on to be a star in high school, Appalachian State University, and the NFL. "I have my mom to thank for it," Dino admits. "But I still never told her about breaking her tree or being banned from playing football in grade school."

BERNIE KOSAR

Quarterback

Cleveland Browns

★ ★ ★

Bernie Kosar thought it would be a snap to play quarterback on his seventh-grade team.

But his very first game turned into a disaster. The first two times the cocky quarterback threw the ball, he was intercepted. In fact, he played so badly that the coach switched him to halfback to teach him a lesson. In the second half, Bernie had to carry the ball on almost every play and finished the day bruised and battered.

Early in his childhood in Youngstown, Ohio, the future Cleveland Browns' star quarterback wasn't allowed to play on any organized teams because his father thought practice took up too much time. So Bernie played pick-up football games and became the best quarterback in the neighborhood. By the time he turned 13 and started seventh grade at Byzantine Central Catholic, Bernie was itching to show everyone how good he really was. "When my dad finally told me I could play on the school team, I was really happy," Bernie recalled. "Now I had the chance to prove to my friends that I was a great quarterback."

In his first game for Byzantine, which had only 12 students on the whole squad, Bernie faced a team that had over 40 members. "I was ready, though," he said. "I knew I could lead our team to victory." Proudly wearing his school football uniform, Bernie took the field for the first time. He surveyed the defense and took his first snap from center. Quickly he back-pedaled, looking for a receiver. Confidently, he threw his first pass downfield. Disaster! It was intercepted!

Bernie came off the field with his confidence slightly shaken. "I knew I'd make up for it the next time," he said. The other team scored and kicked off to Byzantine. Once again Bernie took the field determined to make up for his earlier mistake. He took the snap and retreated to throw a pass—and fired another interception!

Bernie wasn't quite as confident when he came back to the bench this time. "What do you think you're doing out there?" his coach roared at him. "Get your head in the game!" Bernie stood helplessly on the sideline as the other team took advantage of the turnover and scored again. During the rest of the half, Bernie managed to complete a few passes but he couldn't move the offense. Late in the second quarter, Byzantine recovered a fumble close to the other team's goal line. Bernie thought he could right all wrongs by directing his squad in for a score just before halftime. He dropped back, looked in the end zone, spotted one of his receivers, and threw the ball—right into the hands of a defender for Bernie's *third* interception!

Head down, Bernie trudged back to the bench. The coach never said a word until the team was in the locker room at halftime. Then he snapped at Bernie, "So, you want to be a quarterback. But all you can do is throw interceptions! Well, I'm going to let you see what it's like to play another position in the second half. Maybe it will teach you to be a better quarterback if you learn how hard everyone else gets hit on the football field."

When the second half began, Bernie found himself at halfback. "My coach called my number on nearly every play," he recalled. "I was running the ball and getting hit hard the whole second half. I was getting murdered. Every time I touched the ball, two or three bigger guys would hit me.

"I was bruised and battered after the game, but it made me see one thing clearly. I wanted to be a quarterback. I realized that being great in pick-up games didn't prove anything. I would have to work very hard to improve so that I could play on a real team. So I vowed that I would always work hard at being a quarterback—and I've done that ever since."

TUNCH ILKIN

Offensive Tackle

Pittsburgh Steelers

★ ★ ★

Tunch Ilkin played football only after overcoming a painful disease, as well as his mother's intense dislike for the game.

The Pittsburgh Steelers' All-Pro offensive tackle was born in Istanbul, Turkey, and moved with his family to Illinois when he was three years old. The first time his mother, Ayten, saw football she hated it. "My mom thought football was too violent," Tunch said. "She thought only barbarians would play such a rough game."

When young Tunch decided he wanted to sign up for organized football, he first had to convince his mother. "It took a lot to get my mother to agree to let me play," Tunch recalled. "She was against it. But my father, Mehmet, and I double-teamed her. Finally, she agreed to let me join the Midget Football League."

So in seventh grade, Tunch became a running back for the Highland Park (Illinois) Mighty Midgets. It wasn't long before his mother's fears were justified. "I broke the last two fingers on my right hand in one of the first practices," Tunch recalled. "They took me to the hospital emergency room. I was more worried about hiding the injury from my mom than I was about the pain. I kept calling my dad at his office, begging him not to tell my mom." Of course, there was no way to hide the cast on his hand when he came home. His mother wanted him to quit right then, but Tunch's father stepped in and allowed him to continue playing.

Tunch returned to the Mighty Midgets and played running back, linebacker, and defensive back until he graduated from eighth grade. "I was a great runner," Tunch recalled. "I was fast and nearly unstoppable. I thought I'd have a great career as a running back."

But before he could play one down of high school football, he developed a bone growth disease called Osgood-Slaughter's Disease, which is caused when a person grows too quickly. "My knees developed knots under them," he said. "I could hardly walk. I couldn't run." The doctor advised him not to play football in his freshman year at Highland Park High School.

But Tunch was itching to play. His friends convinced him to be the team manager so he could at least be near football. "I didn't last one day," he said. "It hurt too much to be standing on the sideline and watching everyone else play. I wanted to be in there, but I couldn't. So I quit as manager."

Tunch wondered if he would ever again wear a football uniform. Fortunately, by the time football rolled around in his sophomore year, he was completely cured of the bone disease. Once again, Tunch and his father had to double-team his mother before she agreed to let him play football.

Tunch joined his high school team thinking he would return to his position of running back. He was wrong. The coach decided his 6-foot frame and 150 pounds were ideally suited for an offensive tackle. The coach told Tunch he was a born lineman, not a runner. "It was the biggest disappointment of my life," Tunch recalled. "I was devastated when the coach stuck me in the offensive line." But soon the excitement of playing football again overshadowed his dismay. "It was great to come back," he said, "even if I was a lineman. I just loved to play, and it wasn't long before I started to enjoy the position."

But his mom's feelings toward football have never changed. "Even today, she can't stand to watch a game," Tunch said. "She still thinks it's too violent."

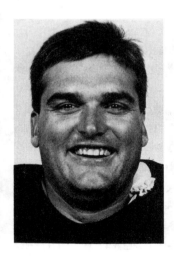

BRIAN BLADES

Wide
Receiver
—
Seattle
Seahawks

★ ★ ★

Brian Blades bullied his teammates so much that his coach benched him for the most important game of the season to teach him a lesson.

The future Seattle Seahawks' All-Pro wide receiver was the star of the Pop Warner League's Western Tigers in his hometown of Fort Lauderdale, Florida. Nine-year-old Brian was a tough defensive back and a speedy running back, who played the game with great intensity. "Brian had a tremendous desire to win," recalled his coach, Johnny Alexander. "He was very intense. He took the game very seriously and insisted that every other team member do the same thing."

Since Brian had far greater skills at this age than the other boys, he harassed teammates when they couldn't play up to his level. Even his own younger brother, Ben-

nie (who now plays for the Detroit Lions), fell victim to Brian's anger when he didn't do something right. "Brian would yell at Bennie or one of his teammates if they didn't live up to his expectations," Brian's mom, Rosa, said. "Brian thought that he was so good he should be able to tell everyone else what to do. He acted like he was a general and everyone else had to follow his orders."

Brian's verbal abuse became worse as the season wore on—and then he started to actually slap boys who didn't perform up to his standards. "I got out of hand," Brian confessed. "When the other boys didn't do something the way I thought they should, I would scream at them. If they did it again, I would slap them. I even slapped my own brother for doing things I didn't like on the football field. I just wanted to shake them up and get them to pay attention."

Brian continued bullying his teammates even though Coach Alexander warned him many times to stop it. Finally, the coach had seen enough. "Brian went too far," Alexander recalled. "He forgot that he was a player and not a coach. It wasn't his role to discipline people. Just because he was the team superstar didn't give him the right to hit, shake, or scream at other players."

At first, Alexander gave Brian the opportunity to apologize to his teammates for his actions. Brian refused. "Brian didn't think he had done anything wrong," his mom recalled. "He believed that he was totally right in disciplining the other players. He believed he could do anything he wanted to do and nothing would happen to him."

Brian was wrong. Coach Alexander benched Brian for the most important game of the season against the Delray Rocks of nearby Delray Beach. "Brian was shocked," his mom recalled. "At first, he didn't believe the coach would do it."

"Brian had to be disciplined," said Alexander. "He had to understand that the key factors in football are personal discipline and team loyalty. You have to follow the rules, and even the superstar has to take orders. The coach runs the team, not the players."

So a stunned Brian sat on the bench and watched as his team lost to the Delray Rocks. Before and after the game, Brian cried his eyes out because he couldn't play. But Coach Alexander stood firm. "We lost when we could have won if we had used Brian," Alexander said. "But the lesson Brian learned was more important than any victory."

To this day, Brian lives by that lesson. "Coach Alexander turned me around," Brian admitted. "He taught me a lesson that I have never forgotten. The team comes first and players obey their coach. The superstar is no different from any other player, and if he thinks he is, then he hurts the team."

DOUG WILLIAMS

Washington Redskins quarterback Doug Williams can take the hardest hit—and get up as if nothing had happened.

"I owe it all to my older brother Robert," Doug said. "When I was a kid, he made me tough. Now when I get up after being hit I think about him. Nothing is as bad as it was playing for Robert."

Robert gave up playing minor league baseball for the Cleveland Indians when Doug entered the seventh grade. Robert returned to Zachary, Louisiana, and became a teacher who also coached the junior high school football team.

"Doug didn't want to play," Robert said. "But I made him." Reluctantly, 12-year-old Doug agreed to play for Northwestern Junior-Senior High School. But he didn't want to be a quarterback. Instead, he joined the junior varsity as a wide receiver. "I didn't like contact," Doug recalled. "I wanted to be a wide out—way, way wide

out where I could beat one guy and not be hit."

Robert didn't see it that way. He made Doug the quarterback and then put him in as middle linebacker on defense. "I didn't have any choice," Doug recalled. "Robert made me play linebacker even though I was skinny and not very tall. I shouldn't have played that position, but Robert wanted me to learn how to hit and be hit." In practice, Robert ran most of the plays at Doug. "I wanted him to make all the tackles," said Robert. "I wanted him to learn to always get up after a hit."

Things weren't any easier for Doug at home. "Robert used to make me play against my brother Larry, who was three years older than me and a defensive tackle on the varsity," Doug recalled. "We went out in the yard and played one-on-one after practice and on weekends. The house was out of bounds on one side and a butane gas tank was the other sideline boundary. Tackles were often made by slamming the other player into the wall or the tank."

Robert's attitude was that you had to be tough to play sports, and he wanted his brothers to be prepared. He kept them playing for hours in the backyard. "Larry was bigger and faster than me," Doug recalled. "He absolutely killed me in those games. I couldn't quit because Robert would whip me if I did. Robert was tough, and he wanted Larry and me to be tough, too. He kept us out there playing in the cold until our noses were running. He didn't let up."

Finally, when Doug and Larry were dragging, Robert let them stop. The next day, they were back out again, banging into each other. "I wouldn't let Doug quit," Robert recalled. "I always told him that athletics were no place for a boy and that he had to be a man to play. He had to be tough. If he walked away, he was a boy, not a man."

Although he was hard on Doug, Robert secretly was very proud of his younger brother. "I never let Doug know how proud I was of him," Robert said. "Doug took everything I threw at him and came back for more."

Doug kept at it because he loved and admired his older brother. "Robert taught me to enjoy the game," Doug said. "He taught me to get back up after taking a hit. It was Robert who made me what I am today. Whenever I get hit on the football field, I get back up. And every time I do, I know that Robert is proud of me. I thank him for caring enough to make me tough enough to play."

FREEMAN McNEIL

Running
back
___
New
York
Jets

★ ★ ★

Freeman McNeil almost missed playing in the biggest high school game of his life because he was busy cutting lawns.

Freeman, the star running back for the Banning High School Pilots in Wilmington, California, worked at a part-time job because his family was poor. In fact, Freeman had so little money that the school's boosters bought him a pair of football shoes and a pair of socks to replace the torn, hand-me-down shoes and socks he used to wear. To earn extra money for his family, Freeman cut lawns for his uncle whenever there was no school or practice. But the job nearly cost the future New York Jets' running back his greatest day as a high school player.

"One Saturday, before a big game against our arch rival, Carson High School, my players were all supposed to be dressed and on the bus by noon," recalled Coach Chris Ferragamo. "But

Freeman was late and we didn't know where he was." Ferragamo held the bus as long as he could. Then, just before the coach ordered the bus to leave, Freeman arrived in an old truck loaded with lawn-mowers and grass clippings. Freeman was hot and sweaty and covered with grass and dirt. He apologized to the coach and said that he had been cutting lawns since 5 A.M.

"I was shocked," recalled Coach Ferragamo. "Freeman was our best player and we needed him well-rested for the game. Yet, he'd been working for seven hours before coming to the bus. He had to get suited up on the bus while we were riding to the game. I thought he would be too tired to play his best." Just the opposite was true. Freeman enjoyed his best day ever in high school. He shattered a school record by rushing for 285 yards and led the Pilots to a 35-6 victory.

Freeman hardly looked like a football player, let alone a record-breaking runner when he first showed up for summer practice as a junior at Banning. "Freeman and his brother Russell grabbed the top of the fence and vaulted over it onto the practice field," recalled Coach Ferragamo. "They were dressed in cut-off jeans and carrying raggedy old shoes tied over their shoulders. They said they wanted to play football, so I told them to put on their shoes and get in line."

Before transferring to Banning, Freeman had played offensive guard at another school where there was little coaching. "It was quickly obvious that Freeman didn't know how to play guard," recalled the coach. "He didn't even know how to properly get down in a lineman's stance."

Naturally, Ferragamo wasn't very impressed with Freeman. But all that changed when the coach conducted a drill to see how well the linemen could run. Freeman was the fastest. When Ferragamo learned that Freeman had never run with the ball, the coach put a ball in the boy's hands and told him to try and run past one of the team's best defensive linemen. "Freeman simply dipsy-doodled once and went by the lineman without being touched," recalled the coach. "So I put two linemen against Freeman and he did the same thing. I decided right then and there he was going to be a running back for us when the season started." A month later, in his first game as running back, Freeman dazzled his coach, his teammates, and the fans by running for 145 yards against Loyola High.

Freeman was a leader who always thought of the team first. After making a touchdown, he would ask the coach to give another runner a chance. "He didn't want to play all the time," Ferragamo said. "He wanted everyone on the team to participate. He was the ultimate team player."

Recalled Freeman, "I loved carrying the ball. It was all I wanted to do. But this is a team game and you have to remember that you are just one player. Your teammates deserve a chance, too."

BRUCE MATTHEWS

Offensive Guard
Houston Oilers

★ ★ ★

Bruce Matthews was cut twice in one day from two different Pop Warner teams. "I was too young for one team and too heavy for the other," Bruce recalled. "I couldn't win."

The Houston Oilers' All-Pro offensive guard was nine years old and in fourth grade in Arcadia, California, when he tried out for his first tackle team. But Bruce was too big to play with boys his own age. "I weighed 125 pounds," Bruce said. "The weight limit for my age was 100 pounds. So I was told I couldn't play."

Bruce's dad, Clay Matthews, Sr., knew his son wanted to play football badly. So the same day Bruce was cut, his dad took him over to a team of 11- and 12-year-olds. "Bruce tried out and made the team," his dad recalled. "But when the coach found

out that Bruce was only nine, he wouldn't let him play. Bruce was as big, if not bigger than those kids. But the coach was afraid to let Bruce play because of his age. He thought the older boys would hurt him, so he was cut for the second time that day."

When a deeply disappointed Bruce arrived home, his older brother Clay (who now plays linebacker for the Cleveland Browns) razzed him about being cut. "You're the only Matthews ever to be cut from a football team," Clay kidded. "And you did it twice in one day!"

Bruce decided to take action. "I figured I'd lose 25 pounds and play on the team with kids my age," said Bruce. "I'd show my brother that I could make the team." Like many dieters, Bruce thought it would be easy to lose weight. He barely ate, swam hundreds of laps a day, and ran 50 sprints daily at the local park. "After two weeks of intense exercise and severe dieting, I had lost just two pounds," Bruce recalled. "I realized I'd never lose enough weight to play at 100 pounds. I was really disappointed because I wanted to show Clay that I could make the team.

"Even though I couldn't do anything about my weight or age, it hurt that I was cut from both teams. I had the ability to play, but I wasn't allowed to play." So Bruce had to be satisfied playing pick-up football with his friends in the neighborhood. He never went out for organized football again in Arcadia.

Three years later, when Bruce was 12 years old, his family moved to Kenilworth, Illinois, where he finally got his chance to play tackle football. Bruce weighed 140 pounds and played offensive guard and defensive tackle on the Kenilworth Rebels in the Pop Warner League. He went on to star in high school, then the University of Southern California, and finally the pros.

But Bruce's family doesn't let him forget the problems he had in Arcadia. "My family still kids me about being cut twice," he said. "My brother Clay reminds me that no other Matthews has even been cut once, let alone twice, from a football team."

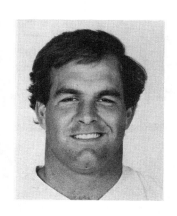

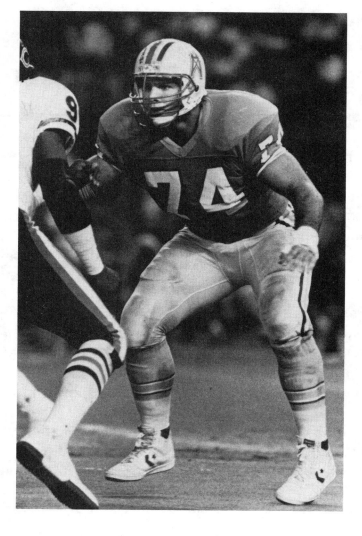

DAN HAMPTON

**Defensive
End**

**Chicago
Bears**

★ ★ ★

Just before he entered the seventh grade, Chicago Bears All-Pro defensive end Dan Hampton suffered a severe injury. He didn't play football again until four years later when he was a junior in high school. And he only played then because the football coach shamed him into it.

Dan started playing organized football in the Midget Football League in Jacksonville, Arkansas, when he was nine years old. By the time he was 12, he weighed 180 pounds and was nearly six feet tall. "I loved football," Dan recalled. "I couldn't wait to get into junior high school and play against better competition."

But then a terrible accident shattered his dreams. Dan was playing with his older brother Matt and their friend, James Pagent, in the meadow in back of his house. "There was a big old tree," Dan recalled. "We had built a tree house 30 feet up. We also had a long rope attached to one of the highest branches on the tree 10 feet above the treehouse.

"One day, Matt and James wouldn't let me swing on the rope and I got mad. I decided I'd get even. I had a knife and I started climbing the tree. I was going to cut the rope while Matt was swinging." As Dan was about to cut the rope, he grabbed a dead limb. "It cracked and I fell 40 feet," he recalled. "I remember the ground coming up very quickly. Then—boom—I hit. I was knocked out for a moment."

At first, Matt thought Dan was faking, so he rubbed a stick in cow manure and shoved it under Dan's nose. "I woke up to an awful smell," Dan recalled. "My left hand hurt very badly, but at first Matt didn't believe I was hurt. I just lay there crying. Then my feet began to swell."

When Matt realized Dan was really injured, he ran to the house to get their mother. She drove the family station wagon to the scene of the fall, loaded Dan in the car, and rushed him to the hospital. Dan had crushed both heels and shattered his left hand. The doctor put pins into his heels, reset his hand, and then put casts on both his legs and his left hand. Dan couldn't walk, and he spent the next five months in a wheel chair. It looked like he would never play football again.

So Dan moved on to another love. He was a natural musician who could play the guitar, saxophone, and other instruments. He grew his hair long and played the saxophone in the school band. He also formed his own rock band.

By the time Dan was in the tenth grade at Jacksonville High, he was the biggest kid in school, at 6 feet 4 inches and 235 pounds. It was obvious this school's football team, the Red Devils, could use him because it was losing most of its games. The closest Dan came to football was performing at the halftime with the marching band.

One night as Dan was coming onto the field at the halftime of a game in which the Red Devils were losing 43-7, football coach Bill Reed stopped him. Recalled Dan, "The coach looked me in the eye and growled, 'Why are you in the band? Why aren't you helping us on the football team? Are you afraid?' He gave me the meanest stare anybody had ever given me. Then he stormed off with a disgusted look."

From that moment on, the coach started to work on Dan to return to football. Dan became ashamed that he wasn't playing. "I decided to return in my junior year," Dan recalled. "It was very hard. I didn't know the proper techniques and I was hopelessly out of shape. Besides, pain was a very real thing for me. My feet still hurt." With the encouragement of his friends, family, and the coach, Dan stuck with it and became the team's best player in his senior year.

The experience has served him well in his pro career. "When I made the effort to come back to football, I learned that I could handle pain," said Dan, who has undergone ten knee operations as a pro. "If I could come back from having my heels shattered, then I can come back from anything. You can always overcome an injury if you have the right mental attitude and work hard."

TIM GOAD

Nose Tackle

New England Patriots

★ ★ ★

Tim Goad was the perfect lineman, but he wanted to run the football. The future New England Patriots' nose tackle pestered his grade school coach into starting him at running back once—but Tim was so embarrassed by his play that he never asked to carry the ball again.

Tim went to Red Bank Elementary School in his hometown of Claudeville, Virginia. But his school wasn't big enough to have a football team. So Tim's dad drove him eight miles each day to play for Coach Ed Nester at Blue Ridge Elementary School in nearby Ararat.

From the time he was eligible to play in the third grade, Tim proved he had the heart for football. Even though he didn't weigh enough to meet the minimum league weight standards, Tim conned his way onto the team. "I used to shove rocks in my pockets," he admitted. "When the coach weighed me, he thought I was heavier than I really was. It was the only way he would let me play."

But Tim grew during the next three years. By the age of 12, he was a 5-feet 10-inch, 160-pound offensive and defensive lineman. On defense, he was good. But on offense, he was awesome. "Tim was our right offensive guard," Coach Nester recalled. "We ran almost every play his way and he opened holes so wide that you could drive a car through them. He was great.

"He was perfectly designed to be a lineman. While Tim was fast, he had a lineman's quickness rather than a running back's speed. However, he thought he'd be a great running back." At every practice, Tim begged for a chance to run the ball. Coach Nester was impressed with the boy's desire, but he was reluctant to let Tim play at running back.

"Finally, we gave in," the coach said. "We decided to play Tim at fullback. He was big and strong, so we thought he might be hard to tackle." In the sixth game of the season, against the Stuart Elementary School Wildcats, Tim lined up at fullback for his undefeated Blue Ridge Bulldogs. He was happy to finally get his chance, and he intended to show what he could do.

"Early in the game, I was used only as a blocker," Tim said. "It was a very tight defensive game. Neither team could score." Tim's number was finally called. He took the handoff from the quarterback and hit the line at full speed. "Two little boys grabbed my right leg," Tim recalled. "I was dragging them and trying to shake them off. Then another little boy wrapped himself around my left leg. They couldn't get me down and I just kept dragging them forward."

While Tim was showing off his strength, another small Wildcat player stripped the ball cleanly from Tim's arms. Frantically, Tim tried to reach the defender who had stolen the ball, but there were three Wildcat players holding his legs. With tears rolling down his cheeks, Tim helplessly watched the Wildcat thief scamper 30 yards for what would be the only touchdown scored that day. "We lost the game on that play," Coach Nester said. "Tim was so embarrassed he didn't know what to say. We moved him back to the line and he never asked to be a running back again."

Said Tim, "On one play, I learned that my coach knew what he was doing. I was a lineman, not a running back. After losing the ball in that grade school game, I never even thought about going against my coach again. It taught me that the coach knows best."

SHAWN LEE

Tampa Bay Buccaneers nose tackle Shawn Lee didn't play organized football until he was a sophomore at Erasmas Hall High School in Brooklyn, New York. He found high school football less violent than the street game he had been playing for years.

"I used to play 'smash-face' football in city streets and vacant lots," Shawn recalled. "After I got into organized football and learned the proper way to play, I couldn't play in the streets anymore. It was too violent for me."

Shawn started playing football in his neighborhood when he was ten years old. Because anyone who wanted to play could join in the game, he often found himself up against 22-year-old men. "It was wild," Shawn said. "We took it very seriously. There were no rules. The games were extremely physical."

The field was either a paved street lined with cars or a vacant lot littered with bro-ken glass, bricks, dog manure, boards, and hard-packed earth. Metal gratings and light poles were considered part of the playing field. "Tacklers would knock you into parked cars," Shawn said. "You would be smashed into a light pole or thrown down against a grating. If you were in the clear for a touchdown, the opposing players would do anything to stop you. You weren't even safe after you scored. Someone would almost always grab you and sling you to the ground."

Skinned legs and arms were common. Scars were a badge of honor. "I carry scars on my legs today that I received playing on the streets," Shawn said. "Players were often knocked out and occasionally guys had to be taken to the hospital."

When his neighborhood challenged other neighborhoods, each team rounded up the nastiest players they could find—often men in their 20s. Few players wore any equipment other than one or two players who had helmets. "You had to stuff sweatshirts under your shirt to give you some protection," Shawn said.

Shawn was 5 feet 6 inches tall and weighed 200 pounds when he was 11. But in the street games, he often found himself up against much bigger men. "I often played against a guy we called Lurch," Shawn said. "He was 20 years old, 6 feet 4 inches tall, and weighed 260 pounds. Plus he was mean. He once threw a kid against a heavy metal grate when he made a tackle. His favorite way to tackle was to clothesline you."

Still, Shawn played in the games because they were fun. It didn't matter if it was raining or snowing, the game went on.

Despite his prowess on the streets, Shawn never thought about playing organized football until he was forced to play. The football players at his high school hung out under two enormous concrete arches that flanked the school's entrance. The players would stand there and size up the students, then decide who they wanted to try out for the team. "It was one of the school's traditions," Shawn said. "When they told you to come out, you showed up for practice the next day. You were intimidated into playing.

"One day I was walking under the arches and several football players came up to me. I was a sophomore who was 5 feet 11 inches tall and weighed 220 pounds. The football players ordered me to come out for the team." Shawn reported for practice and found he had the ability to play. He also found it was much less violent than the street game.

"Street football gave me the proper mentality," Shawn said. "But I didn't know the rules of real football. Everything you did in the streets was a penalty in organized football. I never knew tackling with the head and spearing were illegal."

Shawn learned the rules and became a star. "After I became good at organized football, I once tried to play in the streets again," he recalled. "It was too rough for me."

STEVE YOUNG

Eight-year-old Steve Young couldn't believe his eyes. Right in the middle of a game, his mother charged out of the stands, raced onto the field, and scolded a player who had just knocked Steve flat with an illegal tackle.

"It was embarrassing," recalled the San Francisco 49ers' veteran quarterback. "I've never lived it down."

It happened when Steve was a fourth grader playing with the North Mianas Indians in Greenwich, Connecticut. As a swift halfback, Steve carried the ball a lot and opponents had a hard time stopping him.

During this unforgettable game, the Bell Haven Buzzards assigned a player to shadow Steve everywhere on the field. Whenever he had a chance, the defender would tackle Steve around the neck even though it was against league rules. Since the referee hadn't called a penalty, the defender continued to do it throughout the game. This made Steve's parents very upset. His father, who was nicknamed "Grit" because of his toughness when he played football at Brigham Young University, sat in the stands and watched his son take the punishment. But Steve's mom, Sherry, wasn't nearly as calm. "Several times I complained to the referee about that boy neck tackling Steve," Mrs. Young recalled. "The referee just ignored me!" She was afraid that Steve would get hurt from the vicious tackling.

At the start of the fourth quarter, Steve swept around left end and his Bell Haven shadow made yet another vicious neck tackle, knocking Steve flat and momentarily stunning him. "I looked up from the ground," recalled Steve. "I was shaking my head, trying to clear out the cobwebs. I could see that my dad had come down to the sidelines and then stopped. He didn't step on the field.

"Suddenly, I watched in horror as my

mom came storming onto the field, heading right for the guy who tackled me. I was very embarrassed because I wasn't sure that my mom should be on the field at all. The next thing I knew, my mom had the guy in her hands and she was shaking him. It was ugly," Steve said with a laugh.

Mrs. Young was so angry with Steve's tackler that she actually picked him up, shook him, and yelled, "Don't you ever neck tackle my son again!" Then she shook him several more times. Finally the startled boy muttered that he wouldn't do it again. "I put him down and marched back to the stands," Mrs. Young recalled. "Everyone was totally shocked. Afterward, Steve banned me from going to his games. Years later, he finally relented and let me attend them again."

Said Steve, "I had to put a leash on my mom. I had to tell her not to come anymore. I'll tell you what, though. After that incident, when my mom gave my friends an order, they jumped. If she said it was time for them to go home, they went home."

Steve has never lived down the incident. "My friends would mess with my mind after that. Every time I would get hit hard in football, someone would look to the sidelines and say, 'Is your mom coming out now, Steve?' Even today, if a friend of mine sees me take a hard hit in a football game on TV, he will telephone my mom at home and say, 'Steve just got hit pretty hard, Mrs. Young. You better get out there. He needs you.' My friends will never let me forget that my mom once rescued me on the football field."

JOHN ELWAY

Quarterback

Denver Broncos

★ ★ ★

Alost mouthguard nearly cost John Elway his big break in football.

When the Denver Broncos' quarterback was a sophomore at Granada Hills High School near Los Angeles, he was a third-stringer on the varsity. "I didn't plan on using John at all that year," recalled his coach, Jack Neumeier. "He had a great arm, but he needed a good year to learn our complicated offense. So I was just going to let him play in the junior varsity games."

But all that changed when Granada Hills lost its first four games of the year and was trailing 14-0 midway in the fifth game. "I was so fed up with my two quarterbacks that I decided to put John in the game," said Neumeier.

When the coach ordered him in the game, John was shaking with excitement and nervousness. This was his big chance to show everyone how good he was. "It was the first time a sophomore had played quarterback at the high school, so this was a major opportunity," recalled John's dad, Jack Elway.

On his first play, John handed off to the fullback for a small gain. Then the referee blew the whistle, talked to John, and sent him back to the sideline. "No one could figure out why the ref wouldn't let John play," said his dad. "Then we found out what happened. John had been so excited after being told to get into the game that he dropped his mouthguard and lost it on the sidelines. He didn't realize he didn't have his mouthguard when he went out onto the field. After he ran his first play, the refs noticed John wasn't wearing his mouthguard and they wouldn't let him play without it."

So Coach Neumeier called time-out and told all his players on the sidelines to search for the missing mouthguard. "John was looking frantically under the bench, under the equipment, and all over the place," said his father. "Still, no one could find it. Finally, the coach had to put in the quarterback that John had replaced."

Just when it seemed John had lost a golden opportunity, his twin sister, Jana, came to the rescue. She ran down from the stands and searched the sidelines. In a flash, she found the mouthguard lying in the grass at about the 20-yard line. "She raced over to John and a big grin spread across his face when she gave the mouthguard to him," said Jack Elway. "He put it in his mouth and then went back into the game. He was determined to make the most of this opportunity."

And he did just that. John threw two touchdown passes, spearheading a thrill-ing come-from-behind 21-14 victory. From then on, he started every game for Granada Hills until he was injured midway through his senior year. He led his team to the playoffs in his sophomore year and the league championship the following season. Overall, he completed 60 percent of his passes, threw for 49 touchdowns and was the most highly recruited high school player in the country in 1979.

"In a lot of ways, his sister Jana was responsible for him getting that opportunity to show what kind of a quarterback he was," said his father. "John wouldn't have gotten back into that ballgame if she hadn't found his mouthguard. Thanks to his sister, though, he got the chance to shine . . . and the rest is history."

JOEY BROWNER

Defensive Back

Minnesota Vikings

★ ★ ★

Minnesota Vikings All-Pro defensive back Joey Browner started playing football using old rolled up socks for a ball as soon as he was old enough to walk.

"My mother just didn't like the sport," said Joey. "She didn't think football was worth investing money in, so my brothers and I had to roll up bunches of socks to use as a football. My mother wanted her boys to study, not play a game that any roughneck could play."

Yet Joey and his five brothers—Ross, Keith, Willard, Jimmy, and Gerald—were born to play football. All of them played major college football; Joey, Ross, Keith, and Willard made it to the NFL.

"My mom's attitude made things difficult," said Joey. "My brothers and I developed our skills by playing with each other." Growing up in Warren, Ohio, the Browner boys would roll 12 pairs of socks together to make a football. Then they played their own version of tackle football in the house until their mother kicked them outside. "Joey and his brothers were always running into lamps and tables," his mom, Julia, recalled. "They crashed into the walls while tackling each other. The sock football was thrown wildly and Joey or one of his brothers always made diving catches onto my sofa. They kept playing until I threw them out."

The sock football game moved to the yard at the side of the house. "We drew up plays on the ground and then ran them," Joey said. "We pretty much figured out the game by ourselves because our mother didn't allow us to watch much sports. About the only time we ever saw any football was when (former Cleveland Browns and Miami Dolphins wide receiver) Paul Warfield was on TV. My mother went to school with him and she always liked to watch him play. If it wasn't for him, we wouldn't have seen any football."

Joey's mom wished her boys would stop playing football. "I didn't like all the kids piling on each other," she said. "I didn't like the rough stuff because I didn't want my kids to get hurt. I wanted them to be scholars and gentlemen. But I couldn't very well stop the kids from playing around the house. After all, kids will be kids."

Joey and his brothers may never have played football in school if someone hadn't told Mrs. Browner that football was a means to getting a free college education. "My mom became convinced that football was all right only after she learned about college scholarships," said Joey. "She reluctantly let us play organized football, but we had to keep our school grades up. School always came first with my mom."

At the age of ten, Joey joined his first Pee Wee League team, the Little Raiders, and played offensive guard. That started Joey on the path that would lead him to stardom in the NFL. "All of the time that we played on the side of the house with those rolled up socks, none of my brothers ever thought we would all play college football, and that some of us would become pros. All we wanted to do was have fun. Whenever football may drag a little today, I look back on those days and it helps me remember that football should always be fun."

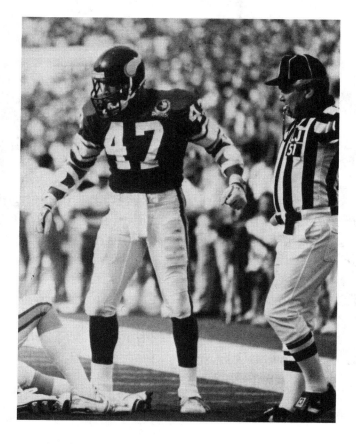

CARL BANKS

Carl Banks was in the clear and about to score the first touchdown of his football career when a defensive back half his size stopped him cold.

"To this day, I'm totally embarrassed by it," said the New York Giants' bruising linebacker. "The guy was a midget. Yet he knocked me down like I was a sack of wheat. I could hear everybody in the stands laughing."

Carl was a large kid when he was growing up in Flint, Michigan. He played tight end and defensive end for the Daily Elementary School Tigers. At 12 years old, he was already 5 feet 8 inches tall and weighed about 140 pounds. Because he was so big, Carl was used mostly as a blocker on offense. "We had a great team," he said. "No one could beat us and we easily made it into the city championship game.

"We ran the ball a lot. It was just as well because I wasn't much of a receiver. I didn't catch the ball that well. We did use a lot of trick plays, though. Everyone got a chance to carry the ball and try to score. I just had never been able to get into the end zone."

Carl was about to have his first and best opportunity to run the ball across the goal line. It came during the championship game against the Zinc Elementary School Mustangs. The Tigers had the ball on their own 10-yard line on third down with the

Mustangs ahead by one point late in the fourth quarter.

The Daily quarterback brought the Tigers to the line of scrimmage. They were in a two-tight-end formation, with Carl on the right and teammate Terry Rushing on the left. The ball was snapped, and the quarterback handed it to the fullback, who started around left end. He handed it to Terry who was coming back the other way. "I counted one thousand one, one thousand two, one thousand three, and turned around," said Carl. "As Terry ran by me, he handed me the ball and I took off around left end." It was a double-tight-end reverse—and the Mustangs fell for it completely! It looked like Carl would score a touchdown on a dramatic 90-yard run.

"I was in the clear," he recalled. "There was nothing but open field ahead of me. I was going to score and then spike that ball as hard as I could." But one Zinc defensive back wasn't fooled. The smallest guy on the field, Duane Thomas, ran down the opposite sideline, cut across the field, and stood waiting for Carl on the Mustangs' 5-yard line.

"This guy was so small I could hardly see him," said Carl. "There was no way he was going to stop me from scoring. I was so big I thought I could run right over him." But Duane was a lot tougher than Carl thought. Fearlessly, Duane charged Carl, rolled himself into a tight ball, and hit him with all the force he could muster. Down went Carl, five yards short of the goal line. "He flipped me completely over," said Carl. "It was totally embarrassing."

Carl lost his big chance to score. The Tigers failed to punch the ball into the end zone, and they lost the game by one point. To this day, Carl has never forgotten the incident. "It taught me a lesson. I never underestimate an opponent. It showed me that a guy might be small in stature, but he can be very tough inside. From that moment on, I have respected every player I've played against. I realize that he is playing hard and I had better be prepared or else I'll end up lying embarrassed on the field again with everybody in the stands laughing."

DERON CHERRY

Defensive Back

Kansas City Chiefs

★ ★ ★

Nine-year-old Deron Cherry was inspired by the saying "When the going gets tough, the tough get going." These stirring words were spoken by his football coach, Osa Meekins, during a halftime pep talk in a game in which Deron's team was losing badly and had completely given up.

"I have lived my life by this motto," Deron said. "To me, it means when you are facing adversity, you have to keep working to overcome it. You never give up."

The future All-Pro defensive back for the Kansas City Chiefs played for the Little Pals of the Garden State Midget Football League in his hometown of Palmyra, New Jersey. Deron played quarterback and his brother, Duane, who was a year older, was a running back. Both were defensive backs as well on a team that went undefeated in their first five games. Then they played Palmyra's biggest rival, the Fairview Raiders. It was a rainy,

dreary Saturday when the Little Pals, dressed in full uniform, boarded the bus for the drive to nearby Fairview.

The first half, played on a muddy field in a driving rain, was a nightmare for Palmyra, who fell behind 38-0. When the half ended, Deron and his teammates had their heads down as they walked off the field. "Mr. Meekins ordered us into the bus and out of the rain," recalled Duane. "He didn't care that we were tracking mud in the bus." The assistant coaches came on the bus and tried to talk to the players while Meekins stood outside. "No one was listening to the coaches," Deron recalled. "Some players were crying, others were looking out the window. All anyone could think about was that we were going to lose."

Coach Meekins could see the boys' expressions through the bus windows. Suddenly, he came storming onto the bus and ordered the assistant coaches to wait outside. Grimly, he shut the bus door. "You aren't losers!" Coach Meekins yelled. "Quit acting like losers. Pick your heads up and look me in the eye!" The team had never seen their coach so angry. Heads snapped up and players sat riveted to their seats. "This is no time to give up!" he yelled. "Quitters never win and winners never quit." Then Coach Meekins uttered the words that Deron has never forgotten. "When the going gets tough, the tough get going," the coach said. "It's time to dig deep down inside yourselves and find what you're made of." Recalled Deron, "He was very emotional. What he said touched me deeply. He didn't care that we were losing. But he did care that we had given up and were sitting there with our heads down."

The speech inspired Deron and the rest of the Palmyra team. "We were a different team in the second half," Duane recalled. "We came out fighting. We all reached down and got that something extra Mr. Meekins had talked about." Palmyra stormed back and racked up seven touchdowns in the second half while holding Fairview scoreless. However, Fairview still won 38-35. But Palmyra had won a moral victory. And Deron had been given a motto for life.

"It has stuck in my mind," Deron said. "Life is full of adversity. When you get knocked down, you have to get back up. You have to be willing to pay the price regardless of the circumstances." Deron is where he is today because of this motto. Football experts had labeled him too small and too slow to be a pro defensive back. "But they didn't consider the toughness I have inside me," Deron said. "I was willing to work hard to achieve my goal."

Deron dedicated a football season to Meekins when the coach died a few years ago. "I'm where I am today because of Mr. Meekins," he said. "He was a coach who cared about developing me as a person. He cared more about his players than he did about winning. Mr. Meekins will always be an inspiration to me."

ANTHONY MUNOZ

Offensive
Tackle
—
Cincinnati
Bengals

★ ★ ★

Future Hall of Famer Anthony Munoz suffered the most mortifying tackle ever—when his pants were pulled down to his ankles in front of the whole school!

Anthony never played tackle football until he was in high school, but the Cincinnati Bengals' All-Pro offensive tackle did participate in flag football in junior high. And that's when he experienced his most embarrassing moment on the gridiron.

Anthony was in eighth grade at Imperial Junior High School in Ontario, California, at the time. He was class president and also the president of the school's chapter of the National Honor Society. "We started a program to try to get all the kids involved in school," Anthony said. "Each homeroom received points for attendance, involvement in clubs and activities, and athletics. The members of the student council were the captains of the homerooms."

Anthony was the quarterback of his homeroom's entry in the school's flag football league which played its games on the school playground during lunch hour. His team made it to the championship game, which was played over two days—one half each day. Anthony and his fellow players were dressed in gym shorts, T-shirts, and sneakers. They each had two flags tucked into a belt around their waist. "I was the biggest kid on either team," said Anthony, who was already over 6 feet tall and weighed about 200 pounds.

The first half of the game ended in a tie. The next day, the whole student body surrounded the playground to watch the final half of the game. "It wasn't very long into the second half when I tried to sweep around the end," Anthony said. "A tackler came after me and I tried to lean away from him. He made a desperate lunge at my flag. Fortunately, he missed. Unfortunately, he grabbed my shorts instead and pulled them down."

Suddenly, Anthony was standing in front of the whole student body with his shorts around his ankles! "My face turned red," Anthony recalled. "I was totally embarrassed. It seemed like there were 100,000 fans jam-packed around that field." To make matters worse, Anthony was a very shy boy. He had difficulty standing in front of the school to make his speech when he was running for class president. Now, he was standing with his pants down in front of those same classmates.

"That's when I discovered I had a very fast reaction time," Anthony said. "I dropped the ball and pulled up my pants at lightning speed!" He tried to remain cool and shrug it off. But the other kids were laughing out loud and he could see everyone was looking at him. "I ran back to the huddle as fast as I could," he said. "My teammates were grinning, but no one said anything to me. I called the next play and we just went on playing." Oddly enough, his schoolmates never mentioned it to Anthony again. "That's because I was bigger than them," he said.

Anthony went on to star at Imperial High School, the University of Southern California, and the NFL. But he's never forgotten the incident in junior high school. "It definitely was the most embarrassing moment of my football career."

DARRYL HENLEY

Defensive Back
———
Los Angeles Rams

★ ★ ★

When Darryl Henley was a young football player, he was so nervous and scared before big games that he would cry.

The future Los Angeles Rams defensive back grew up in Duarte, California, but played in the Pop Warner League for a team called the Gremlins in nearby Arcadia. In his second year with the Gremlins, nine-year-old Darryl was an established star, averaging two touchdowns a game. But he had a problem. He still became very frightened before big, important games.

That became clear when his team made it to the play-offs and had to face the Pasadena Bulldogs, the toughest team in the league. The Bulldogs had handed the Gremlins their only defeat during the regular season. "It was the biggest game of my life and all I could think about was that

we were going to lose," said Darryl. "I was so scared."

A week before the game, Darryl's mother, Dorothy, decided she'd better do something to help clear his mind. "I gave Darryl a book about positive thinking," she recalled. "I wanted him to read it and think about what it said. Then he could try to use it to solve his problem." The book was Norman Vincent Peale's *The Power of Positive Thinking*. Although it was written for an older reader, Darryl finished it and understood it. "After reading the book, I thought I could do anything," Darryl recalled. "I was very confident. I felt I could control my life."

But as Darryl approached the field before the game, his fear returned. "I started crying," he said. "I didn't want to play. My mom had to come down and put her arms around me and convince me to play. She told me to think about the book. I did. I went out and played the best game of my life because of that book." Darryl scored two touchdowns in his team's 25-0 victory. In fact, he played so well that fans from the opposing team picked him up and carried him over to their sidelines where he received a standing ovation.

Arcadia then played against Azusa for the league championship. His team had easily defeated Azusa earlier in the season. "I knew we would win," Darryl said. "I wasn't even scared about playing in the game. Azusa wasn't as good as my team." But Darryl and his teammates were overconfident. Azusa played hard and whipped Arcadia 14-10. "Azusa wanted the championship more than we did," Darryl said. "We thought Azusa would roll over and play dead because we beat them once. Instead, Azusa never gave up and beat us.

"That game taught me something," Darryl said. "My team was better, but we lost. You should never think you are too good because you're setting yourself up for a loss. You have to respect the other team and always treat your opponent as if he could beat you. That's a lesson I've never forgotten.

"I still get nervous before big games. But I always remember that I can do anything if I just believe I can."

KEITH BYARS

Running Back

Philadelphia Eagles

★ ★ ★

When Keith Byars was a youngster, his brothers called him "Momma's big baby" and forced him to play football. They made him compete against older kids in neighborhood games just to toughen him up.

Growing up in Madison Township, a suburb of Dayton, Ohio, the future Philadelphia Eagles' running back was discouraged from playing football by his parents because they didn't want him to get hurt. That was just fine with Keith.

"Keith was a quiet, polite boy," said his mother, Margaret. "He hated violence and he didn't like to fight, which is what often happened during neighborhood football games. He used to tell me, 'If there's a fight, I'd rather walk away.'"

However, even though Keith didn't particularly like to play football, he loved watching the sport on TV. And he loved playing imaginary football games in his front yard. "He started doing that when he was seven years old," recalled Mrs. Byars. "He pretended he played for the Cleveland Browns. He'd throw the ball up in the air and catch it and then zig zag across the yard. He'd score a touchdown and then pretend he was the crowd and let out a big cheer."

His brothers Russel, who was three years older than Keith, and Reggie, who was two years older, thought that Keith could use a little toughening up. They knew he couldn't get tough playing pretend football. "His brothers used to call Keith 'Mamma's big baby' because he didn't want to play with them at first," said Mrs. Byars. "But Russel and Reggie forced him to play football with the older boys."

The teams, which played on a nearby field, were made up of boys as old as 17 and as young as seven. No one wore any football gear. As the youngest, Keith had trouble competing against the older players. He also had another problem—his brother Russel. "Russ was particularly hard on Keith," said Mrs. Byars. "If Keith cried or did anything wrong on the football field, Russel would hit him. If Keith was hurt or wanted to quit, Russel would hit him. Keith was always coming home with a bloody nose that his brother gave him. But he didn't really complain."

Today, Keith admits that those neighborhood games toughened him up. "They were knock-down-drag-out games," he said. "They were very physical and since there was no age or size limit, anybody could play. You just had to tough it out." While enduring the shouts of "Momma's big baby," and the bullying of his brother, Keith learned how to run sweeps, dives, and draws. He learned how to block, tackle, and take a hit. By the time he entered seventh grade, no one called Keith names anymore, not even Russel.

But when Keith joined the Trotwood Junior High team, there was one thing he hadn't learned. "I didn't know how to put shoulder pads on or how to lace them up," Keith recalled. "I couldn't figure out where the hip and thigh pads went. I had never worn a uniform before, and I didn't want to ask anyone how to put it on. So I just watched the other players and copied what they did.

"When I look back on my childhood today, I wouldn't want it to have been any other way. My brothers—especially Russ—did toughen me up. I'd have them do the same thing to me all over again."

CRAIG WOLFLEY

Offensive Guard

Minnesota Vikings

★ ★ ★

When Craig Wolfley was seven years old in Orchard Park, New York, he told his mother, Esther, a secret. "First, he made me promise not to laugh," Craig's mom said. "Then he leaned close to me and whispered, 'I'm going to be a professional football player when I grow up.'"

Craig, an offensive guard for the Minnesota Vikings after ten years with the Pittsburgh Steelers, knew he would have to be strong to play high school football. So he began lifting weights when he was 12 years old. "I didn't have the weights very long before I had an accident with them," he said.

One night Craig and his cousin Kurt Stiefler were lifting weights in Craig's upstairs bedroom. "I had all 110 pounds of the round weights on the barbell," Craig recalled. "As I lifted the barbell over my head, the round weights started to shift and one fell off, hitting the bare wooden floor with a loud crack."

The bar wobbled back and forth as weights on both sides crashed onto the floor. A stunned Craig was left holding the empty bar above his head. "I looked over at Kurt, who was laughing his head off," Craig recalled. "In his hands were the collars which were supposed to hold the round weights on the bar. I was standing there with a stupid look on my face when my father came bursting into the room screaming."

Craig and his weights were banished to the garage where he continued his workouts each day for an hour after school. But in the winter, the Wolfley's garage, which was not heated or insulated, was cold. "As the days got colder, I started to lose interest in weight lifting," Craig recalled. "I had to wear gloves because the metal barbell was so cold. I could see my breath as I lifted weights."

Craig decided he wasn't going to lift any more weights—and he no longer wanted to be a professional football player. He didn't count on his mother's reaction. "Craig's father had taught him to identify his goal and work hard to achieve it," she said. "He didn't want Craig to quit at anything."

So when Craig tried to come into the warm house, his mother shoved him back into the garage with the encouraging words, "Don't come in until you finish your workout."

"Mom, let me in," Craig pleaded. "It's cold out here."

"If you want to get warm," she said, "lift your weights faster." Then she locked the door so he couldn't come inside.

Desperate to get warm, Craig had an idea. "I was sure she would let me in the house to get a drink," he recalled. "Once I was inside, no one would get me back into the garage to lift weights." But his mom outfoxed him. She opened the door only a crack and handed Craig a glass of water. "Drink it out there and finish your weight-lifting," she said. Then she slammed and locked the door. "I couldn't believe it," Craig said. "My own mother locked me out of the house. I went back to my weights and did my whole workout so she would let me back in."

After that, Craig kept his eyes on his goal. He started playing tackle football when he entered Orchard Park High School. In his freshman year, he was an offensive guard for the Quakers. During his sophomore year, he had a brief stint at fullback. "Coach Harris Weinke gave me a chance to play fullback, but he told me that if I fumbled, I was back in the line," Craig recalled. "In the third game of the season, a defender fell on my right ankle while another hit me in the chest. The ball went flying out of my hands and I had a severely sprained ankle. Two weeks later, when I could play again, the coach had me back at offensive guard."

During the weeks he played fullback,

Craig used to run up the hills near his home with a football tucked under his arm. He weaved in and out through the trees at the top of the hill, pretending to dodge tacklers. "One night I did it when it was dark," Craig recalled. "I was really going fast between the trees until one of them smacked me straight between the eyes. I fumbled then, too. All things considered, I knew I was born to be an offensive lineman."

ANDRE RISON

In his first high school game, Atlanta Falcons wide receiver Andre Rison lined up against his school's arch rivals. With only seconds left in the game, Andre's team was trailing by one point and there was time for only one last desperation pass. Andre raced past his defenders and broke into the clear in the end zone. The pass was thrown perfectly to the wide open Andre. He reached out to make the catch for the winning touchdown—and dropped the ball!

"It tore my heart out," recalled Andre. "I cried for two hours after the game. I was behind everyone just waiting for the pass in the end zone. No defender was anywhere near me. I just dropped the ball."

Andre was one of the most talented sophomores ever to play at Northwestern High School in Flint, Michigan. The local newspaper even nicknamed Andre "Super Soph." Andre was proud of his athletic reputation and he intended to show everyone in his first high school game that it was well deserved. He strutted onto the football field at Flint's Atwood Stadium for the big game against Powers High School. It was a perfect night for football—the sky was clear and the temperature was in the 60s. The stands were full of fans waiting to see "Super Soph" in action.

Mark Ingram (who became a wide receiver with the New York Giants) was the Northwestern High quarterback. "Mark could throw the ball a mile and I could outrun anybody," said Andre. "We had a field day." During the game, the pair hooked up for three touchdown passes—each for over 30 yards. However, the extra point attempts failed after every score.

With only seconds left on the clock, Northwestern trailed 19-18. Tensely, Mark took the team to the line of scrimmage at the Powers' 49-yard line. Andre was split far out to the left. Powers had seven defensive backs on the field—and they were backed up deep to prevent the long scoring pass.

On the final play of the game, Mark dropped back to pass, looking long to Andre. "I broke off the line of scrimmage and the defensive backs started backing up," Andre recalled. "I just ran as fast as I could and then cut to the middle of the field. To my surprise, I was all alone. I broke into the end zone in front of the goal posts, and there wasn't a Powers defender within 10 yards of me.

"I turned around and there was the ball coming to me as big as a balloon. I knew in my heart we had won the game. I could hear our fans starting to cheer. I was getting ready to do my touchdown dance. The ball came down, and went right through my arms, hitting me on the shoulder pads and chest. Then it bounced straight through my clutching fingers and hit the ground. I just stared at the ball as it rolled away. Then I fell to the ground and started pounding it. My heart was broken and I was crying and I couldn't stop. My teammates tried to make me feel better, but I knew that we had lost the game because of me. If I hadn't dropped that crucial pass, we would have won.

"But you learn from your mistakes. I swore that my team would never lose another game because of me dropping a pass. And none of the teams I have been on since then has lost because I've dropped a pass."

While his teammates and his fellow schoolmates may have forgiven Andre for dropping the winning pass against Powers, they certainly didn't let him forget it. When he went to school on the following Monday, Andre couldn't go anywhere without someone playing the song "You Dropped a Bomb on Me."

"My teammates and classmates ribbed me unmercifully with that song," he said. "But they also taught me a lesson. I had to work and concentrate to prevent making any more mistakes like that one. I've done that. I sure wish I could forget that song, though. Even today, my friends will play or sing that song to remind me of the day I dropped the bomb."

BENNIE BLADES

Defensive Back
Detroit Lions

★ ★ ★

Bennie Blades, one of the toughest defensive backs in pro football, first took up the sport because he was afraid of his older sister.

"I was scared to death of my sister, Vylnda, because she used to beat me up," Bennie explained. "She would hit me on the side of the head with her tap shoes when I sat around the house. It really hurt. Finally, I decided that if I was going to get hit in the head anyway, I might as well play football. At least I would be wearing a helmet then."

Bennie grew up in Fort Lauderdale, Florida, with Vylnda, his older brother Brian (who now plays in the NFL), and his younger sister Sonya. Since Vylnda was three years older, she was in charge of the house when Bennie's mother, Rosa, was at work. Brian would go off to play Pop Warner football while Bennie was left at home to do the chores under Vylnda's supervision. Bennie had strict orders to mind Vylnda whenever their mother wasn't home.

Although he was only seven years old at the time, Bennie was actually bigger than his football-playing brother, Brian. Bennie, who weighed about 100 pounds, looked like he was 12 years old. He was big enough for football, but he decided not to play because he didn't want to get hurt. "I didn't like football at all," said Bennie. "Brian loved the game and he would leave the house to play every chance he got. So I was left alone with my sisters.

"Vylnda was taking tap lessons, and she had shoes with metal taps on the soles. She was constantly hitting me in the head with those shoes because she felt I wasn't doing the chores. My younger sister, Sonya, would team up with her, and they would beat me up. One day I just had enough. Brian started to leave the house to go to practice and I asked if I could come along. While I was scared of football, I thought that at least I'd have a helmet on if I got hit in the head."

So Bennie showed up at the practice field, but there was a problem. Although he was big enough, he was too young. The league was for kids 8 through 12 years old. "We made an exception for him because he was so big," said Johnny Alexander, the coach of the West Lauderdale Tigers. "Besides, we knew how much he wanted to get out of his house."

Recalled Bennie, "Mr. Alexander took pity on me. He knew I couldn't stand anymore of the abuse that Vylnda was giving me." So Bennie became a linebacker on the Tigers and started playing football regularly. "In all the time I played, I've never been hurt as badly as Vylnda used to hurt me with those tap shoes," he said. "I can still feel them whapping against the side of my head. Vylnda had no mercy.

"The funny thing is that when I signed my first contract as a professional with the Detroit Lions, I bought Vylnda a BMW with some of my bonus money. I figured I owed her a car. If it hadn't been for her and her tap shoes, who knows what I'd be doing now. I owe my football career to Vylnda."

WARREN MOON

Eight-year-old Warren Moon was hurt and embarrassed when his coach yelled at him, "You stink!" during a Mighty Mites Football League game. Warren swore to himself that no one would ever have reason to say that about him again.

"The coach yelled it so loud that everyone heard it," Warren recalled. "My whole team and everyone in the stands heard the coach say it. It hurt me badly. But it made me determined to be a better quarterback so that it would never happen again."

The future Houston Oilers' All-Pro quarterback lived in Baldwin Hills, California, and played for the Mighty Mite Saracens. Off-duty Los Angeles policeman Joe Rouzon was his coach. "Warren was an outstanding boy," Coach Rouzon recalled. "He used to study hard and play football hard. He was very conscientious. Even as

a very young boy, Warren had all of the leadership qualities necessary in a quarterback." The coach admired young Warren. He saw the potential in the youngster's ability to throw the football. Besides, he thought Warren was a terrific boy whom everyone loved.

But one moment of anger by Coach Rouzon affected Warren deeply, and it has stayed with him all his life. It happened during a game against the Saracens' hated rivals, the Venice Blues. The Saracens were losing 20-18 late in the game when Coach Rouzon called a trick play that took advantage of Warren's great arm.

The ball sat squarely on the 50-yard line as the Saracens broke the huddle on fourth down. Everyone lined up on the left except one wide receiver who had just stepped onto the field at the far right sideline. No one from the Blues noticed him. The ball was snapped and Warren turned quickly toward the receiver standing all alone near the right sideline. Warren threw the ball and the receiver got ready to catch it. His path was clear—it looked like a certain touchdown. But Warren's throw was too high! It sailed three feet over the receiver's head for an incompletion. The Blues took over on downs, and Baldwin Hills lost its last hope for victory.

Warren trudged toward the sideline with his head down only to be confronted by his angry coach. "You stink!" Coach Rouzon yelled at the top of his lungs. The other players and the fans in the stands were shocked at what they heard. Warren was crushed. With tears in his eyes, he walked to the sideline as far away from his coach as he could. He was hurt and badly shaken. "I was crying," Warren admitted. "But through my tears I became determined that no one would ever be able to say I stink again. I swore I would work hard and be so good that no one would ever even think it."

As the game wound down, Coach Rouzon had second thoughts about what he had said to Warren. "It was in the heat of battle," the coach recalled. "I didn't mean it and shouldn't have said it. Warren was a terrific player." The coach walked over to the downcast Warren and put his arm around him. "I apologized to him," Coach Rouzon said.

Although Warren forgave him, he's never forgotten those two words. After quarterbacking the Saracens to back-to-back championships, Warren walked up to the coach and reminded him of the time he said, "You stink!" Recalled Coach Rouzon, "Then Warren asked me if I was proud of him yet. I felt like crying. I told him that I'd always been proud of him and I always would be."

Today, Warren plays his heart out because, he said, "I never again want to hear someone say 'You stink!'"

CHARLES MANN

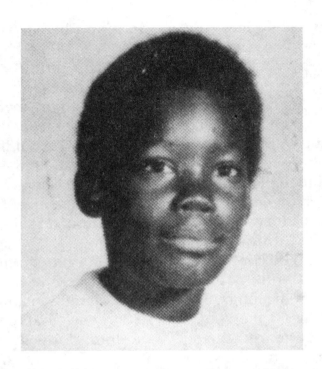

**Defensive
Lineman**
———————
**Washington
Redskins**

★ ★ ★

When Charles Mann was 14, he learned that dealing with mean fans can be as hard as playing against a tough team.

"Some people don't understand what the sport really means," said the Washington Redskins' star defensive lineman. "Some people forget that football is only a game."

Charles was a ninth grader at James Rutter Middle School in Sacramento, California, when he first discovered what it was like to play before a hostile crowd. It happened when his team, the Roadrunners, traveled to the home field of West Sacramento's Broderick Middle School to play a game. "The Broderick fans tried to harass all the teams that came to their field," Charles said. "They tried to scare the opposition into playing a bad game."

A defensive tackle and tight end, Charles stood 6 feet 6 inches tall and weighed nearly 200 pounds, but he still felt intimidated by the Broderick fans. "They crowded around our bus when we arrived to play the game," Charles said. "As we filed into the locker room, they yelled insults and obscenities at us."

In the locker room, Charles's coach tried to settle down the Roadrunners. He told them not to fear the fans. "Coach told us football was a sport that was played on the field, not in the stands," Charles said. "He told us to ignore the fans." Throughout the game, the fans threw bottles and cans at the Roadrunners. "Coach told us to keep our helmets on while we were on the sidelines," Charles said. "He didn't want any of us to get hurt by something thrown from the stands. I got mad. I decided then and there that I wasn't ever going to let fans cause me to lose my concentration and play a lousy game. In fact, because they acted up, my teammates and I played even harder."

Late in the game, James Rutter was

crushing Broderick 43-7. "None of us were going to give their fans the satisfaction of thinking they could scare us," Charles said. "We just focused on playing good, hard, tough football."

But the nasty fans continued to pelt the Roadrunners with junk. "Finally, our coach had had enough," Charles said. "He took a time-out and called the whole team together on the sidelines. He said, 'Fall on the ball and let's get this game over with. Then everybody get together in a group and keep your helmets on while we leave the field.'"

When the final gun sounded, the Road-runners bravely and calmly marched the 500 feet to the locker room through an angry Broderick crowd. "You could see the hate on their faces," said Charles. "I kept wondering why they were so upset. After all, it was only a game."

When the Roadrunners finally entered the locker room, they had a startling surprise. The room was in a shambles. Some of Broderick's fans had torn it apart and stolen everything worth taking. "We were starting to get scared," Charles admitted. "Guys were crying. The Broderick fans were chanting from outside that they were going to do to us what they did to the locker room."

The coach told his players to gather what was left of their belongings and keep their helmets and uniforms on because they were leaving immediately. The Road-runners then raced safely through the hostile crowd to their bus.

"Those fans tried to make life miserable for us," Charles said. "But we rose to the occasion. We weren't going to let ignorant fans ruin the joy of playing football. Sports should always be fun."

BOBBY HEBERT

Quarterback

New Orleans Saints

★ ★ ★

When New Orleans Saints quarterback Bobby Hebert was a boy, he loved football so much that he had to play during the summer. So he organized his own football team.

Twelve-year-old Bobby not only quarterbacked the team, but he coached it as well. He drew up a playbook, ran tough practices, and raised money to equip the team in his hometown of Cut Off, Louisiana.

"I called the team the GPS Hawks," Bobby said. "I ran it like a coach and owner would a professional team." G and P were the initials of property owners on both sides of the street he lived on, and the S stood for suburb. Every boy on the street was drafted by Bobby to play for his team. "Bobby had boys from 6 to 14 years old playing under him," his father, Bobby Hebert, Sr., recalled. "He was a no-nonsense coach. He had those boys out there practicing from dawn to dusk during the hottest months of the summer."

Bobby was a terrific organizer. He raised money from families in the neighborhood to buy helmets and shoulder pads for his team. His practices were as disciplined as any school team. He even went around to other neighborhoods and helped them organize teams so that the Hawks had someone to play. No adults participated in the league Bobby helped form. The boys made their own rules, decided how long the games would be, and called their own penalties.

"It was all his own idea," Bobby's dad said. "No one put him up to it. One day, he decided that he wanted to have a team." Bobby ran that team for three straight summers until he entered high school. "No one ever beat us," recalled Bobby's brother Billy Bob. "We'd play 15 to 20 games a summer and win every one."

Bobby's love of competition inspired him to spend hours studying football plays, strategies, and defenses. "Bobby drew up his own playbook," his father recalled. "Years later when he made the pros, we took out that playbook and compared it to the Saints' playbook. Many of Bobby's plays were exactly the same."

Bobby was a very intense player-coach, Billy Bob recalled. "He ran very tough practices. If you didn't do something right, he yelled at you like any coach would. Sometimes, he'd send kids home crying. Once he criticized a defensive lineman so badly during a game for making a mistake, the boy went home crying in the second quarter. Bobby wouldn't put up with any mistakes."

Bobby even forced Billy Bob to play defensive line once because he had fouled up. At the time, Billy Bob was only six years old and the smallest boy on the team. "I was fooling around and Bobby didn't like it," Billy Bob recalled. "Normally, I played defensive back because I was so small. But to straighten me out, Bobby forced me to play defensive and offensive tackle. I was really scared because I was so small compared to the boys I was playing against." After Billy Bob played well against the bigger competition, Bobby came over after the game and put his arm around his younger brother. "I just wanted to show you what you could do if you concentrated," Bobby told him. "I knew you could handle those bigger boys."

Bobby, who began playing football at the age of four, drove himself as hard as he did the other players on his team. He didn't have any fear of playing against older boys. "Bobby had his collarbone broken playing against older boys," his dad recalled. "But it didn't stop him from playing."

Bobby started the team for the same reason he plays football today. "I love to compete," he said. "I love to play the game. I was the coach because I always wanted to be the leader. I'm a quarterback today because I still want to be the leader."

ANDRE REED

Wide
Receiver
—
Buffalo
Bills

★ ★ ★

The smallest boy on Andre Reed's Knee High football team taught the future Buffalo Bills' All-Pro wide receiver to never give up.

Andre and his teammates were about to quit after falling behind in a championship play-off game. They were crying in the huddle and had already conceded defeat although there were still a few minutes left in the game.

One player refused to quit. He was the team's littlest player—David Jones, who rallied his teammates by promising them they would win the game. "David was the smallest player, but he had the biggest heart," Andre recalled. "He started screaming at us, calling us quitters. By his will alone, he forced our team to play hard and we came back to win the game. For the first time, I saw what it meant to be a team leader who refused to lie down and quit in a game. From that moment on, I tried to follow David Jones' example."

Andre played Knee High football for six years in Allentown, Pennsylvania. His father, Calvin, encouraged Andre and his brothers to play. Since they were not big, they had to rely on speed, quickness, smarts, and physical endurance to compete in football. Calvin Reed used to run his boys until their tongues hung out to make sure they were in shape.

Andre, who played defensive back and quarterback for Allentown, was the star of the team, which had players from ages 8 to 14 who weighed under a certain limit. Andre was also one of the team's lightest players. In fact, when he was 14 and in the tenth grade, Andre weighed only 107 pounds. Yet he led his Knee High team to a 10-0 record.

That year, no opponent scored on Allentown until the big game against the Alton Park Comets. Late in a scoreless contest, the Comets drove the length of the field and scored a touchdown to win 6-0. "Our whole team just broke down," Andre recalled. "We couldn't believe we had been scored on. We were in shock and we didn't know how to react."

Entering the championship play-offs with one loss, Allentown was in a tight defensive battle against Palmer Township. With six minutes left in the game, Allentown's punt returner fumbled on his own 10-yard line. Palmer then took one play to score. "We were stunned," Andre said. "We knew we were going to lose."

Added his brother, Dion, "The players were crying their eyes out. Everyone had given up except little David Jones. He looked Andre in the eye and yelled, 'It isn't over yet. Don't ever give up. We can still win!' Then he turned to the rest of us and gave us a spark. His encouragement and leadership made us believers."

Strengthened by David's words, Allentown took the kickoff and Andre marched his team the length of the field. At the 1-yard line, Andre sprinted out to the right and spotted David in the end zone. David, who played halfback, caught Andre's pass for the touchdown to tie the game at 6-6. In the huddle, David wanted to run the ball in for the extra point—Allentown didn't have a placekicker.

"David was fierce," Dion recalled. "He demanded the ball and promised he'd score. 'We're going to win this game!' he said. Everyone believed him." Andre then handed off to David, who smashed over left tackle for the extra point to win the game. Allentown was now in the finals against Alton Park, the only team to beat them.

"David showed me what leadership was all about," Andre recalled. "I knew that I'd never give up again in a game." And Andre didn't. Once again, the game against Alton

Park was a defensive duel. With only minutes left in a scoreless game, the Comets tried a trick play. Their halfback took the handoff and swept left. Suddenly, he stopped and threw the ball back across the field to the quarterback. Everyone but Andre was fooled.

"I knew it was a pass," Andre recalled. "I ran up, intercepted the ball, and took it 80 yards for a touchdown to give us the victory and the championship."

MARC WILSON

The first time young Marc Wilson played in a championship game he and his teammates nearly drowned.

They had to play the big game in a horrendous downpour that turned the gridiron into a muddy lake. "In some places on the field there were eight inches of water," recalled the veteran New England Patriots' quarterback. "If you got tackled you were more concerned about drowning than fumbling."

Marc was a nine-year-old offensive tight end and defensive end on the Purple Bees in the UNIVAC League in Seattle, Washington. As one of the quickest and fastest players on the team, Marc led the Purple Bees to an undefeated regular season. The team then played for the city championship against Rainier.

Several days before the big game, the rains came and wouldn't let up. Unfortu-nately, the site of the championship clash, Seattle's Inner Bay Stadium, had a field with very poor drainage. By game time, water was covering the gridiron. "When we showed up, we saw that we needed snorkels more than football helmets," Marc recalled.

To make matters worse, temperatures in the 40s accompanied the rain and chilled the players to the bone. "It didn't matter that the field was under water and it was raining," said Marc. "In Seattle, we didn't call off games just because of the rain. The stands were full and we were ready to play."

As they lined up for the opening kickoff, the players were already sopping wet. They felt weighted down by their water-logged shoes and rain-soaked jerseys. The cold, wind-whipped rain numbed their hands. "I didn't care," said Marc. "I didn't even feel cold because I was so excited about playing for the championship."

It looked like anything but a championship game. Because of the horrible weather and awful field conditions, the players kept slipping and sliding in the water and mud. Neither team could mount any kind of an offense. In fact, the Purple Bees scored all their points on defense in the first half when the Rainier quarterback was tackled twice in his own end zone for safeties. At halftime, Marc's team led 4-0.

As the players walked to the sidelines, they began to shiver from the bitter cold and pelting rain. Recalled Marc's dad, Doug Wilson, "Near the field was a railroad overpass. Some parents had gone underneath it and started a fire with some old logs. At halftime, we hustled the kids from both teams under the trestle and near the fire so they wouldn't freeze to death."

The weather conditions worsened in the second half as the wind and rain grew stronger. "The water was so deep on the field that the football floated between plays," said Marc. "The wind kept blowing it away. After every play, the referee had to hold the ball in place."

The Purple Bees' offense simply couldn't get untracked in the second half. Meanwhile, Rainier somehow managed to overcome the wind and rain and scored a touchdown late in the game to eke out a 6-4 victory.

"Even though we lost, it's a game I'll always remember," said Marc. "It was such a thrill to play in a championship game—despite all the water, mud, and cold."

CLAY MATTHEWS

Linebacker

Cleveland Browns

★ ★ ★

An inspirational talk with his father kept future Cleveland Browns All-Pro linebacker Clay Matthews from quitting football when he was nine years old.

"I wanted to give up football because it wasn't any fun and my best friend was going to quit," Clay recalled. "My dad sat me down and told me the importance of always finishing what I had started. If it wasn't for that talk, I might not have played football again."

Clay lived in the small town of Clinton, North Carolina, at the time. There was no organized football league for the town's kids until they got into high school. Because many boys wanted to play football, their parents got together and formed two teams which squared off against each other in six games. "There was no age limit," Clay said. "Everyone could play because there were just enough kids in the town to have two teams." Clay and his friends played full contact football. Their uniforms were blue jeans, sneakers, T-shirts, and helmets.

Clay assumed he would play a glamour position. "I was assigned to play in the offensive line," Clay said. "It wasn't any fun at all. I hated playing that position." So when his best friend, who was also a lineman, decided to quit, Clay thought it was a good idea. "Why play if it isn't fun?" Clay said. "That was the way I looked at it."

Fortunately for Clay, his father, Clay Matthews, Sr., didn't see it the same way. The next day Clay Sr. asked his son why he wasn't going to practice. When Clay told him that he had quit the team, Clay Sr. sat his son down for a talk. "I told Clay that he shouldn't get in the habit of quitting once he started something," his dad said. "If he did that, it would become easy to quit every time something went wrong in the future. A man has to stick to what he starts even if it is tough to do. Besides, he shouldn't quit just because his friend quit. If Clay did that, he could become a follower all his life, doing things because other people did them."

His father left it up to Clay to make the final decision. "I could see my dad was very concerned," Clay said. "I knew he'd be disappointed in me if I quit, so I decided to go back to the team." Clay returned that day to practice and continued playing in the offensive and defensive line, even though he was one of the smallest kids on the team. As he continued to practice, he started to love football.

"I learned it was fun just to play, no matter what position you had," Clay said. "I was just learning the game and it was con-fusing for a kid my age to play on the line. I didn't really understand what was going on, but I learned more every day." His stay at lineman only lasted the first two games before he was moved to running back and linebacker. "My enjoyment of the game grew even greater at these positions," Clay said.

When the family moved to Arcadia, California, the high school coach made Clay a lineman again. This time, Clay didn't complain. "I understood the game well by then and I played it very intelligently," recalled Clay. "The running backs always wanted to follow my blocking because I could open a hole so well." But Clay's life as a lineman ended once again when his coach moved him to outside linebacker—the position he has played ever since.

"Throughout my career I've had difficulties to overcome. But I always think back to what my dad told me when I was nine years old," Clay said. "He instilled in me a sense of commitment. I've never quit anything since our talk."

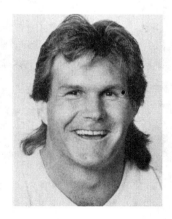

MORTEN ANDERSEN

Twenty-four hours after Morten Andersen saw his first American football game, he was kicking 50-yard field goals for Ben Davis High School in Indianapolis, Indiana.

The future New Orleans Saints' placekicker was an exchange student from Denmark who arrived at the home of his sponsor, Dale Baker, on his 17th birthday on August 19, 1977. Baker was the assistant principal at Ben Davis, and his sons Roger and Dean played football for the school team.

"Morten had filled out a form about himself that I was given before he arrived," Baker remembered. "On the form, it said that he liked football. At the time, I didn't realize he meant the sport we call soccer. I thought he meant American football."

Thinking Morten liked the American sport, Baker and his family took Morten to a football jamboree on the Friday night Morten arrived in Indianapolis. "I was bewildered," Morten recalled. "I had never seen this game before. My American 'father', Dale, was embarrassed about his mistake, but he patiently explained the game to me. I must have asked him two hundred questions. As I watched, I realized that even though I didn't understand the game, I really liked it."

Morten was particularly interested in placekicking. He didn't see what was so difficult about kicking a ball 40 or 50 yards through the goal posts. "By the time the jamboree was over, Morten expressed a real interest in playing the game," Baker recalled. "So I spoke to the coach and he told me to bring Morten to practice the next day."

On Saturday, Morten arrived at practice. His only equipment was his pair of red soccer shoes from Denmark. After giving Morten an old torn blue jersey, the coach showed him the football and how to use a kicking tee. Then the coach stood back to watch what he could do. "Morten calmly started kicking field goals," Baker recalled. "The whole team stopped practice to watch him. He was booting them easily from 50 yards out. The players were bug-eyed. They couldn't believe Morten's kicking ability."

Awed by his kicking, the team accepted Morten immediately. The coach then decided to see what he could do on kick-offs. The team lined up and Morten placed the football on the kicking tee. "I ran up to kick it and crushed it," Morten recalled. "I sent it over 75 yards through the end zone." Morten was given the job as kicker for the Ben Davis Giants and was handed a new purple and white jersey.

The Giants won all 11 of their regular season games and Morten made every one of his extra points.

The Giants were good enough to go to the state championship. In the semifinal game against Evansville Reitz, the Giants scored two touchdowns, but led by only 13-0 because Morten missed his first extra point of the year. It was a kick he'll never forget. "To this day, I know it was good," Morten recalled. "I just kicked it so high the referees were unsure whether or not it went inside the cross bar. One ref called it good, the other no good. After a conference, they decided it was no good." Evansville Reitz came back to score two fourth-quarter touchdowns and win 14-13.

Despite his disappointment, Morten was hooked on football. "At first I wanted to return to Denmark to play soccer," he said. "But after playing a whole season of American football, I loved the game. It's the best game in the world."

PERRY KEMP

When speedy Green Bay Packers wide receiver Perry Kemp was a kid, he was faster than most of his teammates. But he couldn't outrun his mother.

The first time eight-year-old Perry touched the football in an organized game, he ran a kickoff back 85 yards for a touchdown—and a surprise. Perry weaved through the defenders, then broke into the open down the right sideline. "Out of the corner of my eye I saw a flash running stride for stride with me," Perry recalled. "I glanced over and there was my mom! She was running along the sideline, cheering me on. I was so surprised that I almost dropped the football. My mom actually pulled about a stride ahead and hit the goal line before I did!"

That became a regular sight at all of the Hickory Vikings games. With parents and fans standing along the sidelines, Perry would race for a touchdown and his mom, Freda, would run right alongside him cheering all the way. "After the first time I wasn't embarrassed," Perry said. "My mom always did it so I just accepted it. I even came to expect it. She always beat me across the goal line."

Perry grew up in Westland, Pennsylvania, but traveled five miles to Hickory to play football. "Perry was determined and had a lot of faith in himself," his mom said. "He was taught that he could be anything he wanted to be if he just worked hard at it." Perry always worked hard. Because he was a skinny kid, people used to say he was too little to play football. That is, until they saw him play.

Perry averaged two touchdowns a game when he played midget football. "I was faster than anyone else on the field," Perry recalled. "I was also slippery." He was such an exciting runner that fans nicknamed him "Magic." During his games, the people on the sidelines would shout "Magic!" every time he touched the ball. His trademark was running into a big pileup and slipping out the other side like magic. No one knew how he did it.

Every time Perry broke into the open, his mom would be running right alongside him. "It wasn't an official touchdown if my mom wasn't stride for stride with me," Perry said. "Just before the goal line, she would make that little spurt to beat me across the line."

Perry used to kid his mother that she was not only faster, but also stronger than him. "He said that to get out of chores," his mom recalled. "It didn't work. As for being faster, well, I was for years. I used to race Perry and his brother Raymond all the time. Perry couldn't outrun me until he was 14 years old. He was so proud when he beat me in a race. He was finally faster than his mother."

While his mom can't outrun him anymore, Perry knows that she's always watching him and cheering him on during Green Bay Packers games. "Sometimes I can feel her running alongside of me," he said. "I'll glance over to the sideline and, of course, she isn't there. But I know she's rooting for me."

Freda Kemp now sits in the stands, hoping one day to see her son achieve the one goal he's always strived for. "When Perry was eight years old, he told me his goal was to play on a championship team," she said. "He hopes that with Green Bay he will soon reach that goal."

KELLY STOUFFER

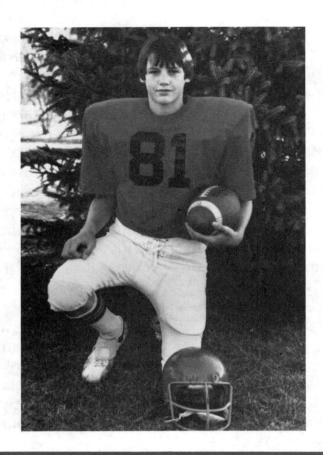

Quarterback

Seattle Seahawks

★ ★ ★

Kelly Stouffer learned to throw accurate passes by spending hours during his childhood tossing rocks at objects in his neighbors' yards.

"When I was in the fourth grade, I began throwing anything that I could get my hands on," recalled Kelly, who grew up in Gehring, Nebraska. "We had a rock bed in front of our house and I would stand there for hours at a time and throw rocks. I'd throw them at targets such as a can or a telephone pole that was 30 yards away. I'd throw rocks across the street or at objects in my neighbors' yards. Sometimes the neighbors weren't too thrilled with all the rocks that wound up on their lawns."

While tossing rocks, the future Seattle Seahawks' quarterback let his imagination run wild and he pretended he was a

football star. "I'd fantasize that I was Joe Namath (Hall of Fame quarterback of the New York Jets). I'd imagine that if I could hit the telephone pole, it would be a touchdown and I'd win the Super Bowl. It was a fun way to pass the time."

Kelly's mother, Shirley, said that she was amazed at how much time he spent throwing rocks from their rock bed. "By the time he reached high school, there wasn't a rock left in our yard. He became so accurate that he never missed hitting his target."

Kelly played another game by himself that taught him how to throw a tight spiral. He would lie on his bed for hours while tossing the ball straight up and catching it. "In the winter in Nebraska, it can get bitterly cold, so I stayed inside," he said. "My parents had a rule that my brothers and I couldn't throw a football around in the house. So I used to go to my room and lie on my bed and throw the ball up in the air. I'd pick a spot on the ceiling and try to hit it with the tip of the ball."

Kelly threw long, accurate passes when he played catch in the backyard with his older brothers Kevin and Craig. But even though Kelly was a super passer, he wasn't given the chance to show off his skills for several years. That's because he was an overweight kid who tipped the scales at 170 pounds in fifth grade. "In pick-up games, I was always the last player chosen so I always had to play in the line," recalled Kelly. "I never played quarterback. But I didn't care because all I wanted to do was play football."

By the time Kelly was 12 years old and in the seventh grade, he still weighed 170 pounds, but he had shot up four inches in height. "Suddenly, my friends didn't tease me about being a roly-poly kid," he said. "Now I was a big kid rather than a fat one."

After the family moved to Rushville, Nebraska, he played running back at Kravath Elementary School. A year later, in the eighth grade, he was given a chance to try out for quarterback. "For the first time, people began to recognize that I could throw the football—and throw it with accuracy," said Kelly. He won the job as the starting quarterback and has never played another position since.

Even though he's an NFL quarterback, he hasn't forgotten his childhood pastimes. Said Kelly, "I might be a professional, but I still spend hours lying on my back, throwing tight spirals up in the air and catching the ball. And when I go for walks, I still pick up rocks and throw them at targets. It keeps me in form."

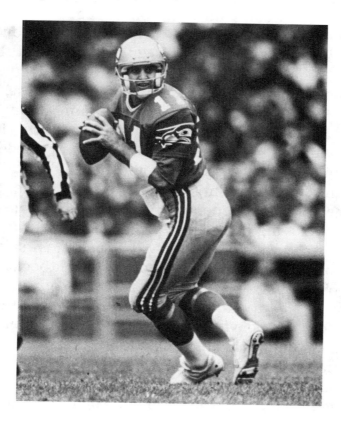

HANK ILESIC

Punter

San Diego Chargers

★ ★ ★

Hank Ilesic lived every boy's fantasy— he actually played pro football while he was still in high school! No one else in North America has ever accomplished that feat.

The Edmonton Eskimos of the Canadian Football League signed Hank to a $17,000 contract when he was 17 years old, just after he completed his junior year. "It was a dream come true," Hank recalled. "I still had one year left of high school eligibility in Edmonton when the Eskimos signed me. I was thinking about playing football my senior year in high school and suddenly I was on a professional team."

The future San Diego Chargers' punter was a great kicker. At 12 years old, he could already punt a football 50 yards. Twice he won the Canadian national Punt, Pass and Kick competition. "I loved the game," Hank said. "I wanted to play at an American university, get a degree, and

then play pro football after I graduated from college."

With his future education in mind, Hank regularly attended the summer developmental camps that the hometown Eskimos ran for local high school and college kids. His booming punts caught the eye of Edmonton coach Hugh Campbell. The Eskimos badly needed a punter and Hank could now boot the ball over 70 yards. "Hugh Campbell told me he wanted me to play for the Eskimos," Hank recalled. "He didn't care that I was still in high school."

The Eskimos' salary offer turned the tide for Hank because he and his mother were living on welfare. His father was dead. "We needed the money," Hank said. "If we didn't, I probably would have refused the offer. I wanted to get an education."

Hank joined the Eskimos shortly after he finished his junior year in high school.

He was 6 feet 1 inch tall and weighed 175 pounds. "I tried to act very mature," Hank recalled. "I was on the same field with my idols. They were all much older than me and most of them were married. The players took me under their wing. If they hadn't, I probably never would have made it. They made sure that I acted correctly on the road and that nothing happened to me."

Hank's first punt came in an exhibition game against Montreal. It traveled 65 yards. In August, he played his first league game at home against Calgary. "It was a very windy day," Hank recalled. "The first official punt I had was blown off the side of my foot and went about 15 yards." That drew a frown from Coach Campbell, who growled, "You'll have to do better than that to play for us. Let's see what you're made of on your next kick." A worried Hank put everything he had into his next punt and it sailed 60 yards. He had no trouble for the rest of the game.

Hank had never been away from Edmonton. His first road trip to Regina, Saskatchewan, was also the first time he had ever been on an airplane. "I was more excited by the plane ride than the football game," Hank said. "I tried to hide it, though, because I didn't want the other players to kid me."

In September, Hank was already a veteran of several Canadian Football League games. But now, with summer vacation over, he had to return to St. Joseph's High School for his senior year. "Some of my classmates were excited for me," Hank recalled. "Others thought I was a traitor because I was playing pro football rather than for my high school."

Throughout the season, Hank went to classes until early afternoon, and then pedaled his bike six miles to make the Eskimos' 3:30 P.M. practice. "I was given a chance," Hank said, "and I made the best of it. I could have flopped and it would have been no one's fault but my own."

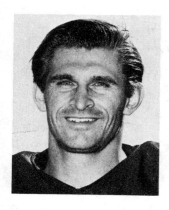

WES HOPKINS

Safety
___
Philadelphia
Eagles

★ ★ ★

Wes Hopkins learned early in his football career that if a team can be intimidated, it can lose to a weaker opponent.

The Philadelphia Eagles' safety was just as tough in elementary school as he is now in the NFL. Wes never knew fear until he was 11 years old and his school played a neighborhood pick-up team in his native Birmingham, Alabama. "My whole team was intimidated," Wes recalled. "We were scared of those boys because they were so tough they played in their bare feet."

Up until then, Wes had demonstrated his own toughness countless times on the football field. He had played games with a broken hand and other injuries. "Wes broke his left hand playing football," his mother, Maggie, recalled. "But he didn't want his coach to know it because Wes knew he wouldn't be allowed to play again until it healed. I had to drag him to the doctor and he put a cast on it. The next thing I knew, Wes had taken the cast off. He went right on playing and the coach never knew he had a broken hand."

His team, St. Francis, was the best in the city's Catholic League, having won back-to-back championships. Wes, a speed demon at running back, had played since he was in fourth grade. "The Catholic nuns used to get the little girl cheerleaders to yell Wes's name," his mother said. "The nuns said Wes would run even faster if he heard his name called. He was the fastest boy on the team and he scored the most touchdowns."

After two straight championships, Coach Quitman Mitchell decided his team was getting too cocky. So he set up a memorable practice game when Wes was 11 years old and just starting sixth grade.

Coach Mitchell took his team to play The Country Boys, a pick-up team from one of Birmingham's poor neighborhoods. The Country Boys had no regular uniforms—they wore what they felt like wearing. Their shirts were different colors and they all wore blue jeans. They had helmets but only a few wore shoulder pads. "The minute we saw them, we were intimidated," Wes recalled. "Most of them didn't wear any shoes. Their field was hard ground littered with broken glass and covered with rocks. It was frightening to face barefoot players who weren't concerned about playing on a field of broken glass. "Our team was scared to death. We wanted to go home, but our coach told us we had to play."

The Country Boys, who attended public elementary schools, weren't any bigger nor any older than the St. Francis players. But Wes and his teammates believed their opponents were tougher because they played shoeless. "These boys were drawing up their plays in the dirt," Wes recalled. "They weren't even a fully organized team. Instead of counting before hiking the ball, they chanted, 'Is everybody happy?' Then they ran their play."

St. Francis hadn't lost a game in two years, but they were slaughtered this time, 50-10. "The Country Boys ran all over us," Wes recalled. "They just dragged us up and down the field. We were probably more talented than they were, but we were too afraid to play our normal game." Wes carried the ball 13 times for a total of minus two yards. "Every time I touched the ball I was looking for a place to fall down," he said.

But Wes learned a lesson for future years. "You should never allow any team or player to intimidate you," he said. "If you're scared, you can't play your normal game. That is how good teams get beat by not-so-good teams."

VINNY TESTAVERDE

Quarterback

Tampa Bay Buccaneers

★ ★ ★

Vinny Testaverde's football career nearly ended before he had a chance to show off his talents on the field.

When he was 12 years old, he temporarily gave up the game because he thought he was "too cool" to play football. Three years earlier, he had been bullied by a couple of mean teammates into almost quitting the team for good.

The future Tampa Bay Buccaneers' quarterback played Pee Wee League football for the Franklin Square Warriors near his home in Elmont, New York. He became such a dominant player that he developed an attitude problem. "I went through a time when I thought I was too cool for football," Vinny admitted. "I quit for almost a week. I didn't go to any practices. Then I wised up. Thankfully, the football coach

accepted my apology and I returned without missing a game."

Vinny never told his dad, Al Testaverde, that he had left the team. Only after Vinny returned did the coach inform the boy's dad of what had happened—and reveal the real reason why Vinny had quit. "Vinny had discovered girls," Al Testaverde said. "He missed practices during the week to hang out in a local mall with his friends and chase girls. As the weekend approached, he had enough sense to return in time to play the game."

That wasn't the first time Vinny thought about quitting football. Three years earlier, two bullies from his own team scared him so badly that he wanted to leave the team. "They were a lot bigger than me," Vinny recalled. "They threatened to hurt me if I didn't quit the team because I wanted to play quarterback." That was the position of one of the bullies.

Vinny had been groomed to be a quarterback by his dad ever since he was a baby. "I put a football in Vinny's bassinet," said Al Testaverde. "I started playing catch with him as soon as he could walk. At the age of four, Vinny could throw the ball as well as any ten-year-old." Vinny was such a good passer that at the age of nine, he was put on the Warriors team which competed in the 12-year-olds' league. "I was much better than the kids my own age," he recalled. "But now I was playing against older, bigger, and more experienced kids."

Vinny, then a tall and shy youngster, found football to be loads of fun—until he joined his new team. "In preseason practice, Vinny was winning the job of quarterback," his dad remembered. "The 12-year-old boy who had been at that position in the past resented Vinny. The boy's 11-year-old cousin also played for the Warriors and they both started threaten-

ing Vinny." The bullies wanted him off the team. Every chance they had, they told Vinny they were going to hurt him if he didn't quit. They threatened him during practice and after practice. Outwardly, Vinny simply ignored them. "But I was really scared," he said. "They were ruining football for me and I thought seriously of quitting. I had to make a decision. My love for football finally won out. I wasn't going to give up the game just because I was being threatened."

Fortunately, the bullies were all talk and no action. They never laid a finger on him. Despite their constant threats, Vinny worked hard at practice and was rewarded by being named the starting quarterback. When the two bullies got the news, they both quit the team.

In his first year as the team's signal caller, Vinny threw six touchdown passes as Franklin Square went undefeated in its nine games. Vinny went on to quarterback the Warriors to four more undefeated seasons.

RON WOLFLEY

As a kid, the Phoenix Cardinals' All-Pro special team player Ron Wolfley would stare at football cards for hours, thinking how wonderful it would feel to have his own bubblegum card.

"I imagined how great it would be to have my picture on one of those cards," Ron recalled. "It would mean I had achieved my goal of making it to the National Football League."

When Ron finally made it to the pros, he experienced a special thrill when he saw his picture on a football card. "The first time I found out that there was a card of me was when a young boy asked me to autograph my football card," said Ron. "He held out the card and I saw my picture on it. Tears started flowing from my eyes. It was a very emotional moment for me because my dream had become a reality."

Football cards gave Ron many hours of fun when he was a boy. He didn't play organized football until junior high in Orchard Park, New York. When he wasn't playing the game in the street, he was enjoying a football card game with his friends on his dining room table. With one player on defense and one on offense, the boys laid out their football cards in a formation. The player on offense then moved the card of his ball carrier until it touched a defender's card for a tackle.

"My friends and I would play for hours," Ron said. "We would smash the cards together to run a play. This was just an example of the love for the game I had even at a young age. I had a vivid imagination and felt I was playing football even though I was only using bubblegum cards."

When Ron wasn't inside playing bubblegum card football, he was outside playing with his friends on Hodson Drive. The boys often challenged another group of kids who lived a half-mile away on Maple Drive. "All of the families on Hodson Drive were poor but the kids from Maple Drive were wealthy and they could afford equipment," said Ron. "Our team didn't play with helmets. I always wore a pair of polyester striped pants and a torn sweat shirt."

The two teams played intense tackle football throughout the year. "It was hard-hitting, tough football," said Ron. "We played all out. Once, I came tearing across the field and intercepted a pass and I cut my knee. Blood was seeping from the rip in my pants, but I didn't care. My friends were concerned, but all I could think of was that this was how real football was played." Ron carries the scar of that game on his right knee to remind him of his childhood.

He also carries the memory of his dad, Ronnie, who died when Ron was 19. "My dad taught me to play hard and give it my best shot," Ron said. "He drove it into my head that I would have to be tough because life wasn't easy."

When Ron was ten, his dad took him to see his first NFL game. It was between the Buffalo Bills and the Pittsburgh Steelers. "What a thrill it was for me," said Ron. "After the game, I stood by the Steelers' locker room because I wanted to get an autograph of (running back) Franco Harris. But when he finally came out, I was in such awe that I didn't approach him. But other kids did. Franco stood there and patiently signed every autograph. His teammates were sitting on the bus, waiting to leave. But Franco didn't care. He stood there and kept signing rather than disappoint a single kid. I'll always remember that. When I'm asked today to sign autographs, I think of Franco and sign every one."

DOUG FLUTIE

As a 12-year-old, a gritty Doug Flutie played in an all-star game with a broken foot.

Doug was a halfback on the South Beach Cubs of the Midget Football League in Melbourne Beach, Florida. All-stars from his league were scheduled to play against all-stars from other midget leagues in Florida to crown a state champion.

One week before the first scheduled play-off game, Doug broke his foot playing football with his younger brother Darren (who grew up to play pro football with the San Diego Chargers). "Darren was only 8 and I was 12, but we played football together every day," said the veteran New England Patriots' quarterback. "I was much bigger than him so I used to play on my knees. Darren would run around and I'd try to tackle him.

"A week before the big all-star game in Deland, Florida, Darren and I were playing football in our bare feet in the front yard. On one tackle, he landed on my right foot and slammed it into the ground. I felt the pain immediately, but I didn't think anything of it. I used to get hurt all the time, and pain never really bothered me that much. So we continued to play. Since I was on my knees, I really didn't notice how swollen my foot had become. When I tried to stand up, I couldn't walk. I didn't want my mom to know that I had hurt myself because she would go crazy over my swollen foot. So I decided I'd sneak into the house and go into the bathroom where I could treat my foot myself."

His mom, Joan, was sitting on the couch reading a book, when she heard a scraping noise. She looked up and saw Doug crawling down the hallway trying to sneak past her. "I asked him what was wrong and he said, 'Nothing,'" recalled Mrs. Flutie.

"When I told him to stand up, he couldn't. I became very upset and ran over to him. I had to pick him up because he couldn't stand. He kept trying to tell me nothing was wrong, yet he couldn't stand up. I had to drag him to the hospital."

At the hospital, Doug received the bad news. He had a broken bone in the top of his foot and he would have to wear a cast for six weeks. Doug was crushed. The all-star game was only a week away and the doctor insisted that Doug couldn't play in the game.

After two days in the cast without playing football, Doug begged his mother to take him back to the doctor and have the cast removed. She said no. "My foot felt fine to me and I didn't think I needed a cast," said Doug. "My mom wouldn't listen, so I went to my dad. I asked him to let me use crutches rather than the cast. He agreed and we removed the cast. My mom was very angry about this, but she had to accept it."

His foot was still badly swollen, but Doug didn't care. He soon discarded the crutches and started walking around. He even played basketball in his driveway. Doug told his parents that he was fit to play in the all-star game even though his foot dragged behind him when he walked.

"Doug begged me to allow him to play," said his father, Dick. "I could see that he didn't have any mobility and wouldn't be able to play halfback. I felt sorry for him because he had worked so hard. I told him he could play if the coach would let him."

Doug practiced for two days before the game and traveled with his team to Deland. Because he couldn't run very well, he didn't get to play halfback. Instead the coach stuck him in the defensive line. "He could hardly move and the other linemen were much bigger, but he made a lot of tackles," Doug's dad remembered.

Doug's team lost, but he had given it his best effort. "Football has always been like that for me," Doug said. "I love the game. Injuries won't keep me from playing."

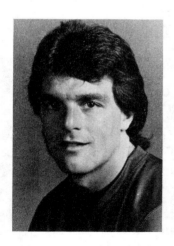

Quarterback

**Dallas
Cowboys**

★ ★ ★

Nine-year-old Troy Aikman decided to play tackle football because he fell in love with a 12-year-old cheerleader and wanted to get her attention.

"I know it sounds crazy," Troy recalled. "Most boys my age didn't care about girls at all. But I was wildly in love with Carla Harkey. She was the reason I started playing tackle football."

The future Dallas Cowboys' quarterback first noticed Carla when he attended a football game in Cerritos, California. His older sisters, Tammy and Terri, were cheerleaders for the Hornets, a team which played in the 13- to 14-year-old Orange County Junior All-American Football League. "I was watching my sisters cheer on the sidelines," Troy remembered. "Then I noticed this long-legged, brown-eyed blonde. She was very peppy and enthusiastic in her black and gold uni-

form. Her long, blond hair was flying around. She was beautiful." When he watched Carla, Troy discovered feelings inside him that he had never experienced before. She interested him more than the football game did.

"After the game, all the older boys from the team gathered around the cheerleaders," Troy recalled. "My sisters and the other cheerleaders were making a big deal over the players. I couldn't get near them. At home later, I overheard my sisters talking about how great football players were. In a flash it came to me: Football players attract girls! Right then, I knew I wanted to be a football player." So Troy decided to go out for the Hornets' 8- to 12-year-old team. "I hoped Carla would notice me if I was a football player," he said.

Troy, who had played flag football the year before, earned the job of quarterback on the Hornets. But he had to face a big challenge before he could play. He was already 5 feet 7 inches tall and he weighed 110 pounds—10 pounds over the weight allowed for his age group. "I was too young to move up to an older team," he said. "If I wanted to play, I had to lose 10 pounds." For the next two weeks, Troy barely ate anything and exercised constantly. "Every time I wanted to quit, I thought of Carla," Troy said. "Finally, at the official weigh-in, I weighed 99 pounds. I had lost 11 pounds." But he was terribly weak. "I would never do that again and I'd recommend that no kid diet that drastically just to make a specified weight," Troy said. "I was sick as a dog and I could hardly run."

Having made weight, Troy started at quarterback. As he had hoped, his sisters cheered for his team and they brought along their fellow cheerleaders. "I thought my dream was fulfilled," Troy recalled. "There was beautiful Carla, cheering from the sidelines. I knew she would be mine soon."

But it never happened. The three-year age difference was too much. Seventh-grader Carla was more interested in boys her own age than a fourth-grader. "I would be on the football field playing and I'd secretly glance over to see if Carla was watching," Troy recalled. 'I loved watching her twirl in her uniform. But she paid no attention to me."

Carla never even knew that Troy had a crush on her. "I never told her," Troy said. "When I was 12, my family moved to Henryetta, Oklahoma. I never saw Carla again. But I still think of her. After all, she's the girl who got me interested in football."

Don't miss the other exciting titles in the little BIG LEAGUERS™ Series!

★ ★ ★ ★ ★ ★ ★ ★ ★ ★ ★ ★ ★ ★ ★ ★ ★ ★ ★

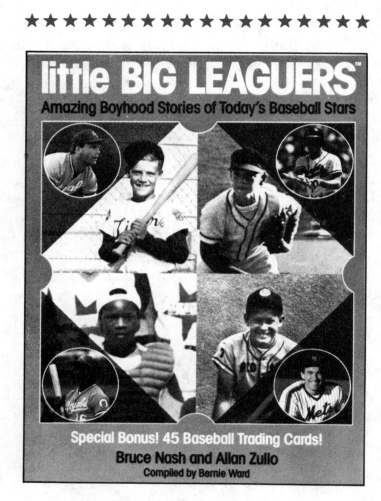

★ ★ ★ ★ ★ ★ ★ ★ ★ ★ ★ ★ ★ ★ ★ ★ ★ ★ ★

COMING SOON!

★ *More* little BIG LEAGUERS™
★ little *Basketball* BIG LEAGUERS™

Dan Marino

little football BIG LEAGUERS™

Roger Craig

little football BIG LEAGUERS™

Rohn Stark

little football BIG LEAGUERS™

Mike Singletary

little football BIG LEAGUERS™

Mike Lansford
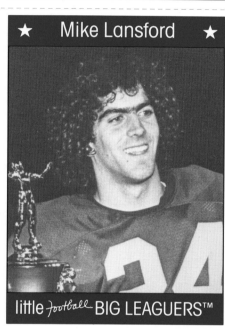
little football BIG LEAGUERS™

Phil Simms

little football BIG LEAGUERS™

Anthony Carter

little football BIG LEAGUERS™

Jerry Ball

little football BIG LEAGUERS™

Bob Golic

little football BIG LEAGUERS™

Rohn Stark

Punter • Indianapolis Colts

Born: May 4, 1959, Minneapolis, Minnesota
Height: 6'3"   Weight: 203 lbs

_____

As a nervous 12-year-old quarterback, Rohn forgot where the plays were designed to go so he had to write the direction of each running play on his hands.

Rohn, who has been to the Pro Bowl twice, is among the all-time leaders in punting with a career average of 44.1 yards.

 little *football* BIG LEAGUERS™

Roger Craig

Running Back
San Francisco 49ers

Born: July 10, 1960, Preston, Minnesota
Height: 6'   Weight: 214 lbs

_____

When Roger was a young boy, he was a real wimp on the football field. On defense, he was so scared of getting hurt that he wouldn't tackle the ball carrier.

As one of the NFL's toughest runners to tackle, Roger set a 49er record with 1,502 rushing yards in 1988. Three years earlier, he became the only player in NFL history to surpass 1,000 yards rushing and 1,000 yards receiving in a single season.

little *football* BIG LEAGUERS™

Dan Marino

Quarterback
Miami Dolphins

Born: September 15, 1961
Pittsburgh, Pennsylvania
Height: 6'4"   Weight: 224 lbs

_____

Dan was cut from his grade school team the first time he tried out. But he was so determined to be a member of the team that he made himself the water boy. Eventually, he quarterbacked the team to back-to-back city championships.

As a Dolphin, Dan broke 16 NFL passing records in his first seven seasons. He was the NFL Rookie of the Year in 1983 and has been named to six Pro Bowls.

little *football* BIG LEAGUERS™

Phil Simms

Quarterback
New York Giants

Born: November 3, 1956
Springfield, Kentucky
Height: 6'3"   Weight: 214 lbs

_____

Baseball was Phil's first love. But when the football coach watched Phil pitch and saw what a strong arm he had, the coach knew he'd make a great quarterback. Then Phil had to be talked into joining the football team.

In 1987, Phil led the Giants to a stunning 39-20 Super Bowl victory over the Denver Broncos. Phil set Super Bowl records for most consecutive completions (10) and highest completion percentage (88 percent on 22 completions in 25 attempts).

little *football* BIG LEAGUERS™

Mike Lansford

Placekicker
Los Angeles Rams

Born: July 20, 1958, Monterey Park, California
Height: 6'   Weight: 183 lbs

_____

In a high school game, Mike suffered from an injured nerve in his kicking leg. So he just turned around and kicked left-footed—and made a game-winning 37-yard field goal.

Mike, the all-time leading scorer for the Rams, racked up 120 points in 1989. He is considered one of the game's best kickers when the game is on the line.

little *football* BIG LEAGUERS™

Mike Singletary

Linebacker • Chicago Bears

Born: October 9, 1958, Houston, Texas
Height: 6'   Weight: 228 lbs

_____

In junior high, Mike was given one chance by his father to prove he could play football well. On Mike's only play in his first game, the ball carrier ran right over him. But since Mike had played the best he could, his dad let him continue.

Mike, who has made seven straight Pro Bowl appearances, was the NFL's Defensive Player of the Year in 1985 and 1988. He anchored the defense for the Bears when they won the Super Bowl in 1985.

little *football* BIG LEAGUERS™

Bob Golic

Nose Tackle
Los Angeles Raiders

Born: October 26, 1957, Cleveland, Ohio
Height: 6'2"   Weight: 265 lbs

_____

When Bob was in grade school, he used to arrive at practice dripping with sweat. That's because his father held a rigorous prepractice for young Bob to teach him the fundamentals of the game.

Bob, a three-time All-Pro, has helped strengthen the Raiders' line. In his best game as a pro, he tallied 11 tackles and a sack against the Indianapolis Colts in 1987.

little *football* BIG LEAGUERS™

Jerry Ball

Nose Tackle • Detroit Lions

Born: December 15, 1964, Beaumont, Texas
Height: 6'1"   Weight: 292 lbs

_____

Jerry had to play his first season of organized football in pants too big for him. So he learned to play with one hand while he used the other hand to hold up his pants.

In 1989, his third year in the NFL, Jerry made the Pro Bowl for the first time. That same year, Jerry set a team record by starting in 44 consecutive games and was named the Lions' defensive MVP.

little *football* BIG LEAGUERS™

Anthony Carter

Wide Receiver
Minnesota Vikings

Born: September 17, 1960
Riviera Beach, Florida
Height: 5'11"   Weight: 175 lbs

_____

Anthony was so good as a youngster that rival teams tried to start fights with him to get him ejected from games. Anthony had to learn to control his temper so he could play.

Anthony, who has played in two Pro Bowls, holds the Vikings' record for most games with more than 100 yards in receptions (15). In 1987, he set an NFL playoff record for most reception yards in a game (227).

little *football* BIG LEAGUERS™

Dino Hackett

little *football* BIG LEAGUERS™

Bernie Kosar

little *football* BIG LEAGUERS™

Tunch Ilkin

little *football* BIG LEAGUERS™

Brian Blades

little *football* BIG LEAGUERS™

Doug Williams

little *football* BIG LEAGUERS™

Freeman McNeil

little *football* BIG LEAGUERS™

Bruce Matthews

little *football* BIG LEAGUERS™

Dan Hampton

little *football* BIG LEAGUERS™

Tim Goad

little *football* BIG LEAGUERS™

Tunch Ilkin

★ ★

Offensive Tackle
Pittsburgh Steelers

Born: September 23, 1957, Istanbul, Turkey
Height: 6'3"   Weight: 266 lbs

————————

To play football, Tunch had to overcome a serious disease and the objections of his mother who thought the game was much too rough.

As offensive captain and the Steelers' best all-around blocker, Tunch was named to the Pro Bowl in 1988 and 1989. He gave up only one sack in all of 1988.

little *football* BIG LEAGUERS™

Bernie Kosar

★ ★

Quarterback
Cleveland Browns

Born: November 25, 1963, Boardman, Ohio
Height: 6'5"   Weight: 210 lbs

————————

Bernie's very first game in organized football was a disaster. The first two times he threw the ball, it was intercepted. In fact, Bernie was so bad at quarterback that the coach moved him to running back to teach him a lesson.

Bernie led the Browns into the play-offs for four straight years from 1986-89. He was ranked fourth among AFC quarterbacks in 1989 when he threw for 3,533 yards and 18 touchdowns.

little *football* BIG LEAGUERS™

Dino Hackett

★ ★

Linebacker
Kansas City Chiefs

Born: June 28, 1964
Greensboro, North Carolina
Height: 6'3"   Weight: 228 lbs

————————

Dino was such a tough but clumsy boy that during a front-yard football game, he plowed into a blue spruce tree—and broke it.

Because of his ferocious style of play, Dino earned All-Pro honors. He has been a starter for the Chiefs since he joined the team as a second-round draft choice from Appalachian State in 1986.

little *football* BIG LEAGUERS™

Freeman McNeil

★ ★

Running Back • New York Jets

Born: April 22, 1959, Jackson, Mississippi
Height: 5'11"   Weight: 209 lbs

————————

Freeman tried out for lineman on his high school football team. But his coach noticed his speed and gave him a tryout at running back. When no one could tackle him in drills, Freeman was made the team's running back.

Freeman, who owns a career rushing average of 4.5 yards per carry, has been the Jets' most exciting runner. He enjoyed back-to-back 1,000-yard rushing seasons in 1984-85.

little *football* BIG LEAGUERS™

Doug Williams

★ ★

Quarterback
Washington Redskins

Born: August 9, 1955, Zachary, Louisiana
Height: 6'4"   Weight: 220 lbs

————————

When Doug was in junior high school, his brother, Robert, coached the team and taught him how to hit and be hit without being afraid. In practice, Robert toughened Doug up by moving him to linebacker and running most of the plays at him.

Doug was named MVP of the 1987 Super Bowl in which he led the Redskins to a 42-10 victory over the Denver Broncos. He set Super Bowl records for most yards passing in a game (340) and in a quarter (228).

little *football* BIG LEAGUERS™

Brian Blades

★ ★

Wide Receiver
Seattle Seahawks

Born: July 24, 1965, Fort Lauderdale, Florida
Height: 5'11"   Weight: 182 lbs

————————

At the age of nine, Brian bullied his teammates so much that his coach benched him for the most important game of the year just to teach him a lesson. Brian learned the hard way that he couldn't hit or yell at the other players just because they weren't as good as he was.

In 1989, his second year in the NFL, Brian caught 77 passes for 1,063 yards and earned a trip to the Pro Bowl. In 1988, he led all rookies with eight touchdown receptions.

little *football* BIG LEAGUERS™

Tim Goad

★ ★

Nose Tackle
New England Patriots

Born: February 28, 1968, Claudville, Virginia
Height: 6'3"   Weight: 280 lbs

————————

Tim was a natural lineman who begged his coach to let him play running back. When Tim finally got his chance, a smaller player stripped the ball from him and ran for a touchdown. Tim was so embarrassed that he never asked to play that position again.

In 1988, his first year with the Patriots, Tim made 32 solo tackles and was named to the NFL's All-Rookie team. He won an award as the Patriots' top lineman.

little *football* BIG LEAGUERS™

Dan Hampton

★ ★

Defensive End
Chicago Bears

Born: January 19, 1957
Oklahoma City, Oklahoma
Height: 6'6"   Weight: 270 lbs

————————

Dan—the biggest kid in his high school—played in the marching band at halftimes until the football coach shamed him into trading music for football in his junior year.

Despite undergoing ten knee operations, the five-time Pro Bowl end has played in more NFL games than any current Bear. One of football's fiercest pass rushers, Dan leads the team in career sacks with 78.

little *football* BIG LEAGUERS™

Bruce Matthews

★ ★

Offensive Guard
Houston Oilers

Born: August 8, 1961, Raleigh, North Carolina
Height: 6'5"   Weight: 293 lbs

————————

Bruce was cut twice in one day when he was nine years old because he was too heavy for one league and too young for another in Arcadia, California.

Bruce is a two-time All-Pro who anchors the Oilers' offensive line. He was a first-round draft choice in 1983 after a sparkling college career at the University of Southern California.

little *football* BIG LEAGUERS™

Shawn Lee

little *football* BIG LEAGUERS™

Steve Young

little *football* BIG LEAGUERS™

John Elway

little *football* BIG LEAGUERS™

Joey Browner

little *football* BIG LEAGUERS™

Carl Banks

little *football* BIG LEAGUERS™

Deron Cherry

little *football* BIG LEAGUERS™

Anthony Munoz

little *football* BIG LEAGUERS™

Darryl Henley

little *football* BIG LEAGUERS™

Keith Byars

little *football* BIG LEAGUERS™

John Elway

Quarterback
Denver Broncos

Born: June 28, 1960, Port Angeles, Washington
Height: 6'3" Weight: 215 lbs

After John's first play in high school, the ref ordered him off the field because John had lost his mouthguard. His twin sister then came down from the stands and found it on the sidelines. John went back to the field and threw two touchdown passes to win the game.

From 1987-90, John led the Broncos to three Super Bowl appearances. In 1989, the scrambling, tough quarterback threw for 3,051 yards and 18 touchdowns.

little *football* BIG LEAGUERS™

Steve Young

Quarterback
San Francisco 49ers

Born: October 11, 1961, Salt Lake City, Utah
Height: 6'2" Weight: 200 lbs

Eight-year-old Steve was embarrassed when his mother came charging onto the field to confront a boy who had just tackled him around the neck. His mother warned the boy never to do it again.

As the back-up quarterback to Joe Montana, Steve was particularly valuable in 1988 when he led the 49ers to several victories while Montana was injured. Steve's leadership helped drive his team to the Super Bowl.

little *football* BIG LEAGUERS™

Shawn Lee

Nose Tackle
Tampa Bay Buccaneers

Born: October 24, 1966, Brooklyn, New York
Height: 6'2" Weight: 290 lbs

Up until high school, Shawn played "smash face" football in the streets of Brooklyn where tacklers knocked runners into parked cars and light poles. When he finally learned the proper way to play, he didn't participate in street games anymore because they were too rough.

In 1989, Shawn recorded 21 tackles and one sack for Tampa Bay. He also had 29 quarterback pressures, the second most on the team.

little *football* BIG LEAGUERS™

Deron Cherry

Defensive Back
Kansas City Chiefs

Born: September 12, 1959
Palmyra, New Jersey
Height: 5'11" Weight: 203 lbs

In Midget League, Deron's team was losing 38-0 at halftime and had given up. But then his coach gave the players an inspirational speech which Deron has never forgotten: "When the going gets tough, the tough get going." His team stormed back with seven straight touchdowns in the second half.

Deron, who's been to the Pro Bowl six times, leads the NFL in career interceptions among active players with 43.

little *football* BIG LEAGUERS™

Carl Banks

Linebacker • New York Giants

Born: August 29, 1962, Flint, Michigan
Height: 6'4" Weight: 235 lbs

At the age of 12, Carl was in the open going for the first touchdown of his career. But the smallest player on the field brought him down near the goal line. Carl's team never did score and lost the game.

The veteran linebacker's fierce desire to win has made him one of the Giants' toughest defenders. His bone-crunching tackles have earned him Pro Bowl honors.

little *football* BIG LEAGUERS™

Joey Browner

Safety • Minnesota Vikings

Born: May 15, 1960, Warren, Ohio
Height: 6'2" Weight: 210 lbs

Joey started playing football using old rolled up socks for a ball as soon as he was old enough to walk. He played with his five brothers, including three who wound up playing in the NFL.

Joey, who anchors the Vikings' pass defense, has made five straight trips to the Pro Bowl. He was named the Defensive Player of the Year for defensive backs in 1988.

little *football* BIG LEAGUERS™

Keith Byars

Running Back
Philadelphia Eagles

Born: October 14, 1963, Dayton, Ohio
Height: 6'1" Weight: 238 lbs

As a kid, Keith was called "Momma's big baby" by his older brother, Russel, who thought he wasn't tough enough to play football. So Russel forced Keith to play against older neighborhood kids to toughen him up.

Today, Keith is one of the Eagles' top rushers and receivers. In 1988, he was the team's second-leading receiver, rusher, and scorer while leading the Eagles with 1,222 total yards from scrimmage.

little *football* BIG LEAGUERS™

Darryl Henley

Defensive Back
Los Angeles Rams

Born: October 30, 1966
Los Angeles, California
Height: 5'9" Weight: 170 lbs

As a kid, Darryl was so scared before big games that he would cry. To remedy this, his mother gave him a book about the power of positive thinking. It helped Darryl gain confidence in himself and he became a better player.

Darryl was a punt returner and a nickle back in his first year with the Rams in 1989. He returned 28 punts for an impressive 9.5 yard average.

little *football* BIG LEAGUERS™

Anthony Munoz

Offensive Tackle
Cincinnati Bengals

Born: August 19, 1958, Ontario, California
Height: 6'6" Weight: 278 lbs

In a flag football game played in junior high, Anthony was running with the ball when a defender lunged at Anthony's flag. Unfortunately, the guy grabbed Anthony's shorts and pulled them down. Anthony found himself standing in front of the entire student body with his shorts around his ankles.

Considered the best left tackle in football, Anthony has been selected to the Pro Bowl nine straight years. He was named the NFL's best lineman in 1981, 1986, and 1988.

little *football* BIG LEAGUERS™

Craig Wolfley

little *football* BIG LEAGUERS™

Andre Rison

little *football* BIG LEAGUERS™

Bennie Blades

little *football* BIG LEAGUERS™

Warren Moon

little *football* BIG LEAGUERS™

Charles Mann
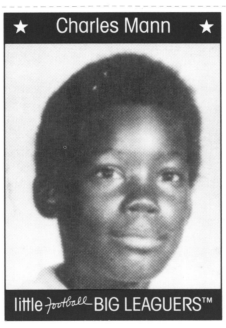
little *football* BIG LEAGUERS™

Bobby Hebert

little *football* BIG LEAGUERS™

Andre Reed

little *football* BIG LEAGUERS™

Marc Wilson

little *football* BIG LEAGUERS™

Clay Matthews

little *football* BIG LEAGUERS™

Bennie Blades

Defensive Back • Detroit Lions

Born: September 3, 1966
Fort Lauderdale, Florida
Height: 6'1" Weight: 221 lbs

Bennie decided to play football because it was safer than staying home with his sister. She used to hit him over the head with her tap dancing shoes whenever he didn't do his chores.

The third player picked in the 1988 draft, Bennie was named to the NFL's All-Rookie team. He averaged over 100 tackles a year in his first two pro seasons.

little football BIG LEAGUERS™

Andre Rison

Wide Receiver
Atlanta Falcons

Born: March 18, 1967
Muncie, Indiana
Height: 6' Weight: 191 lbs

When he was a sophomore, Andre dropped the winning touchdown pass in the big game against his high school's arch rival. Andre vowed he would never drop an important pass again.

As a rookie in 1989, Andre led the Indianapolis Colts in receiving with 52 receptions for 820 yards. Because of his outstanding speed and sure hands, Andre was named to the NFL's All-Rookie team.

little football BIG LEAGUERS™

Craig Wolfley

Offensive Guard
Minnesota Vikings

Born: May 19, 1958, Buffalo, New York
Height: 6'1" Weight: 269 lbs

When Craig was 12 years old, he began lifting weights in the garage so he could get strong enough to play football. Once, when he decided to quit working out, his mother locked him out of the house until he finished pumping iron.

Craig, who played ten years with the Steelers before joining the Vikings, helped keep pass rushers off Pittsburgh signal caller Bubby Brister during the team's surprising march to the play-offs in 1989.

little football BIG LEAGUERS™

Bobby Hebert

Quarterback
New Orleans Saints

Born: August 19, 1960, Galliano, Louisiana
Height: 6'4" Weight: 210 lbs

At the age of 12, Bobby organized his own neighborhood football team and became its player-coach. When he reached the pros, he saw that the Saints' playbook contained plays that were like the ones he had drawn up for his neighborhood team.

Bobby led the Saints to their first play-off appearance in team history in 1987. A year later, he set a club record by completing 87 percent of his passes (20-29) in a game against the Denver Broncos.

little football BIG LEAGUERS™

Charles Mann

Defensive Lineman
Washington Redskins

Born: April 12, 1961, Sacramento, California
Height: 6'6" Weight: 270 lbs

Fourteen-year-old Charles feared for his safety when he and his teammates were threatened by a crowd of mean, vicious junior high school fans. During the game, the fans hurled debris at the players and ransacked their locker room.

Charles made the Pro Bowl three consecutive years in 1987-89. As one of the Redskins' top pass rushers, Charles spearheaded the defense for Washington's Super Bowl championship team in 1987.

little football BIG LEAGUERS™

Warren Moon

Quarterback • Houston Oilers

Born: November 18, 1956
Los Angeles, California
Height: 6'3" Weight: 210 lbs

As a kid, Warren was deeply embarrassed when his coach yelled, "You Stink!" after he had blown a sure touchdown play. Warren vowed to play so well that no one would ever have the opportunity to say that to him again.

After starring in the Canadian Football League for six years, Warren joined the Oilers in 1984. He's now second on the team's all-time passing list. His bullet passes and scrambling style earned him trips to the Pro Bowl in 1989 and 1990.

little football BIG LEAGUERS™

Clay Matthews

Linebacker
Cleveland Browns

Born: March 15, 1956, Palo Alto, California
Height: 6'2" Weight: 245 lbs

Clay was going to give up football because his best friend was quitting the team. But Clay's dad convinced Clay to finish what he started.

Clay, who has played in five Pro Bowls, averaged 86 tackles per season from 1978-89. He recorded 113 tackles, including 84 solo, and four sacks in 1989.

little football BIG LEAGUERS™

Marc Wilson

Quarterback
New England Patriots

Born: February 15, 1957
Bremerton, Washington
Height: 6'5" Weight: 205 lbs

As a kid, Marc once played a championship game in a driving rain storm. With the field under a foot of water in some places, the referee had to hold the ball between snaps to keep it from floating away.

Before joining the Patriots in 1989, Marc directed the offense for the Los Angeles Raiders and threw for 300-plus yards six times, including 367 yards against the Denver Broncos in 1987.

little football BIG LEAGUERS™

Andre Reed

Wide Receiver • Buffalo Bills

Born: January 24, 1964
Allentown, Pennsylvania
Height: 6' Weight: 190 lbs

When Andre was 14, he and his teammates were about to quit after falling behind in a play-off game. But the smallest boy on the team told them to never give up. Andre and his teammates were so inspired they rallied to win.

The two-time Pro Bowler led the Bills in receiving from 1985-89. In 1989, he caught 88 passes for 1,312 yards and had nine touchdown receptions.

little football BIG LEAGUERS™

Morten Andersen
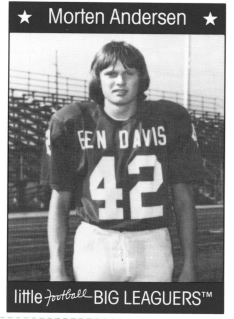
little *football* BIG LEAGUERS™

Perry Kemp

little *football* BIG LEAGUERS™

Kelly Stouffer

little *football* BIG LEAGUERS™

Hank Ilesic

little *football* BIG LEAGUERS™

Wes Hopkins

little *football* BIG LEAGUERS™

Vinny Testaverde

little *football* BIG LEAGUERS™

Ron Wolfley

little *football* BIG LEAGUERS™

Doug Flutie

little *football* BIG LEAGUERS™

Troy Aikman

little *football* BIG LEAGUERS™

★ Kelly Stouffer ★

Quarterback
Seattle Seahawks

Born: July 6, 1964, St. Cloud, Nebraska
Height: 6'3"   Weight: 210 lbs

_____

Kelly learned to throw perfect spirals by playing catch with himself for hours while lying on his bed. He also developed his accuracy by throwing stones at tin cans and telephone poles.

In 1988, Kelly threw for 370 yards against the New Orleans Saints to set a NFL rookie passing record which has since been broken.

little *football* BIG LEAGUERS™

★ Perry Kemp ★

Wide Receiver
Green Bay Packers

Born: December 31, 1961
Canonsburg, Pennsylvania
Height: 5'11"   Weight: 170 lbs

_____

Perry was fast as a youngster, but not as fast as his mother. When young Perry would break loose on a long run, he'd look to the sideline and see his mother running step for step with him.

Perry has turned into one of the Packers' exciting new deep threats. In 1989, he had 48 receptions for 611 yards, an average of 12.7 yards per catch.

little *football* BIG LEAGUERS™

★ Morten Andersen ★

Placekicker
New Orleans Saints

Born: August 19, 1960, Struer, Denmark
Height: 6'2"   Weight: 200 lbs

_____

Morten, an exchange student from Denmark, met his host family in Indianapolis on his 17th birthday and saw his first American football game that night. The next day, he was kicking 50-yard field goals for the local high school team.

Morten, the leading scorer on the Saints, has played in four Pro Bowls. He is the NFL's most accurate field goal kicker among active players with a percentage of .782.

little *football* BIG LEAGUERS™

★ Vinny Testaverde ★

Quarterback
Tampa Bay Buccaneers

Born: November 13, 1963, Brooklyn, New York
Height: 6'5"   Weight: 215 lbs

_____

Threats from two bullies on his own team almost ended the football career of nine-year-old Vinny before it began. But his love for the game overcame his fear of them and he continued playing.

Vinny, winner of the Heisman Trophy in 1987, was the first player chosen in that year's collegiate draft. In 1988, Vinny enjoyed his greatest day as a pro throwing for an amazing 469 yards against the Indianapolis Colts.

little *football* BIG LEAGUERS™

★ Wes Hopkins ★

Defensive Back
Philadelphia Eagles

Born: September 26, 1961
Birmingham, Alabama
Height: 6'1"   Weight: 215 lbs

_____

When Wes was 12 years old, his championship team played a ragtag neighborhood squad that was so tough its members played barefoot on a field loaded with broken glass. Wes and his teammates were intimidated and lost badly even though they were the better team.

As a brainy, hard-hitting safety, Wes is a two-time All-Pro and a leader of the stingy Eagles defense. In 1988, he had a career high of 146 tackles.

little *football* BIG LEAGUERS™

★ Hank Ilesic ★

Punter • San Diego Chargers

Born: September 7, 1959, Edmonton, Canada
Height: 6'1"   Weight: 200 lbs

_____

Hank played pro football with the Edmonton Eskimos of the Canadian Football League before he even entered his senior year in high school.

In his first year in the NFL in 1989, Hank, who kicked for a 40.1-yard average, became known for his high, booming punts which made returns nearly impossible. Eleven of his punts were downed inside the 20-yard line.

little *football* BIG LEAGUERS™

★ Troy Aikman ★

Quarterback
Dallas Cowboys

Born: November 21, 1966, Cerritos, California
Height: 6'3"   Weight: 220 lbs

_____

Troy started playing tackle football at age nine because he was in love with a 12-year-old cheerleader and he thought he'd get her attention by playing football.

Troy, the first player chosen in the 1989 collegiate draft, was so impressive in preseason that he became the starting quarterback for the Cowboys. He set an NFL record for passing by a rookie when he threw for 379 yards against the Phoenix Cardinals.

little *football* BIG LEAGUERS™

★ Doug Flutie ★

Quarterback
New England Partriots

Born: October 23, 1962
Manchester, Maryland
Height: 5'10"   Weight: 175 lbs

_____

At the age of 12, Doug broke his foot playing football in his yard right before an all-star game. Doug was such a tough competitor that he took the cast off his foot and played in the big game anyway.

Doug was named the Heisman Trophy winner in 1984 after setting the record as the all-time NCAA passing leader with 10,759 yards. In 1988, a year after joining the Patriots, the small but gritty quarterback was named the team's Unsung Hero.

little *football* BIG LEAGUERS™

★ Ron Wolfley ★

Fullback • Phoenix Cardinals

Born: October 14, 1962, Blaisdel, New York
Height: 6'   Weight: 222 lbs

_____

As a boy, Ron and his friends spent hours playing with football cards. He always dreamed that one day he would have his own picture on a card.

Now he does. Ron made the Pro Bowl four straight years from 1986-89 for his aggressive play on kickoffs. In 1987, he was voted Special Teams Player of the Year.

little *football* BIG LEAGUERS™